Dear Readers,

One of the nicest thing[...]
is the burgeoning of a multitude of bl[...]
soms we're cultivating in our newly seeded garden
of love. Four of them have burst into bloom this
month, just in time for a fabulous fall flowering.

Take a woman hiding, under an assumed name,
in a small Maine town, and a man hiding from life
itself; add the rescue of a couple of cute kids, and
you have Wendy Morgan's debut romance, **Loving
Max.**

Grab a bikini and head for the tropics. Roast beef
meets tofu when flower child Tasha and button-
down salesman Andrew Powell III meet at a singles
resort in Maddie James's rollicking romance, **Crazy
For You.** Then, in Michaila Callan's **Love Me Tender,**
travel to small-town Texas, where Eden Karr employs
a handsome carpenter to redesign her boutique . . .
and gets a new design for living and loving as well!
Finally, fly to faraway, fantastical Caldonia, where
New York magazine editor Nicole is hired to find a
queen for handsome Prince Rand—before the end
of the year—in **The Prince's Bride** by Tracy Cozzens.
Will his coach turn into a pumpkin before her mis-
sion is accomplished . . . or will love find a way?

Speaking of pumpkins, we'll be back next month
with four splendid new Bouquet romances—in brilliant fall colors. Look for us!

The Editors

LOVE ME TENDER

Eden clenched her hands. The need to touch Jace sizzled in the tips of her fingers, screamed in the hollow of her heart. His hair caught in the neckline of the tunic. Desire won out over reason. She reached up to free the strands.

Black satin slid over her fingers. The stubble on his jaw grazed her wrist. She touched his cheek, ignoring the sirens in her mind. Wrong or right, this connection mattered more than her next breath.

Jace's eyes grew sleepy, seductive. He mirrored her action, his palm rough against her cheek. So easy. So natural. So simple to move the one short step into his arms.

Thunder rumbled low. The sky had darkened, breaking the spell. As much as she longed to do otherwise, she moved back. "Sounds like your hour's been cut short."

Jace seemed indecisive, hesitant, even, like what had just passed between them had confused him as much as it had her. Like he couldn't put a name to the thick tension in the room without calling it what neither of them wanted: involvement, attraction, the beginning of attachment.

LOVE ME TENDER

MICHAILA CALLAN

Zebra Books
Kensington Publishing Corp.
http://www.zebrabooks.com

ZEBRA BOOKS are published by

Kensington Publishing Corp.
850 Third Avenue
New York, NY 10022

First Printing: October, 1999
10 9 8 7 6 5 4 3 2 1

Printed in the United States of America

ONE

The chime above The Fig Leaf's front door rattled, clanked, clattered and moaned—a shopper's welcome with all the appeal of tomcats on the prowl. Cellular phones in a movie theater. Disco music. Labor pains.

Eden Karr pushed aside the scarf section, shoved up her glasses and rubbed the pinched bridge of her nose. The few items of her own design sold in the shop depended on attention to detail. Her attention. Undivided and constant.

The chime had to go. But not today. Right now she was doing good to thread a needle. She wasn't about to try and climb a ladder, toolbox in hand—not when she'd barely managed to roll her pregnant body out of bed this morning.

So much for the joys of self-employment and home ownership, she wryly mused, weighing the benefits of small-town Texas life against the one she'd left behind in New York.

Lifting her foot from the serger's footfeed, she adjusted the unevenly gathered Indian cotton bunched beneath the needle. A spasm shot down her right leg. Inhaling sharply, she knotted her fist and pushed against the small of her back.

Carrying these two babies was already painfully exhausting—especially since, at four months, she was already painfully large. Judging by her burgeoning belly, the twins seemed destined to be born the size of Sumo wrestlers—not that anyone else seemed to notice any of this.

"Yoo-hoo, E-e-e-den."

Dear, sweet Molly Hansen. Smiling, Eden laid her glasses aside and flicked off the machine. Molly's timing couldn't have been more perfect. Eden was way past ready for a break.

"Back here, Molly." She pushed to her feet just as the older woman bustled into the sewing room Eden had painted white and decorated with curtains, cushions, lampshades and watercolors in her favorite shades of purple and green. "Mmm. What's that I smell?"

The wicker basket caught in the crook of Molly's elbow bounced against her slim hip. She lifted the red-checkered dishtowel tucked around the basket's contents. "I've brought honey bran muffins and fresh peach jam. I figured you busied yourself sewing so early this morning that you forgot to eat."

Eden patted her barely rounded belly, covered in a chic maternity tunic of canary yellow. She'd determined early in this pregnancy that chic and maternity were not going to be mutually exclusive. "Now, Molly. I look like I've swallowed a basketball. Do you truly think I forgot to eat?"

"If you've swallowed anything, it's a tummy full of

self-pity. Now come eat." And that was Molly: no-nonsense, no fluff and absolutely no fat jokes.

Wearing one of Eden's newest creations, the older woman breezed down the hallway to the kitchen. Eden followed, critically eyeing the jumper loosely fitted to Molly's frame.

Not bad if Eden did say so herself, studying the apples appliquéd around the hem of the blue and white ticking. Especially since the pattern was such a huge departure from anything she'd designed since college.

Her ideas had leaned more toward Dolce and Gabanna than mom and pop. But this was what Molly had wanted. And the fit, the material, the pattern . . . everything was perfect.

Maybe Eden's worries were all for nothing. Maybe change was going to be a good thing. After all, it hadn't taken but a day to fall in love with this house, Eden admitted, glancing toward the front door, through which her guest had arrived.

The hundred-year-old frame building nicely fit her needs, with her living quarters on the second story and her kitchen and sewing room at the rear of the structure's first floor. What had once been a foyer, a parlor, a living room and a dining area had been remodeled into a storefront that was amazingly ideal.

And speaking of storefront . . . Eden checked her watch. The Fig Leaf was due to open in an hour. Where had the morning gone? Following Molly into the airy white kitchen at the back of the house, Eden lifted a blue enamel teakettle from the stove.

"Here. You sit. Let me do that." Molly left the basket on the table and hurried to finish the task. "No need to put yourself out for me."

While Molly set the kettle to boil, Eden wrapped one arm around her friend's shoulder and hugged her. "I'm not putting myself out for anyone but myself—and the behemoths that have taken over my body." She caressed the right side of her belly and received a flutter of a kick in return. "Yes, oh impatient Benjamin. I'll have two muffins if it will make you happy."

"And how do you know that wasn't Bethany?" Molly raised a skeptical brow.

Eden patted a minor bulge to the left of center. "If it was, she was only practicing her arabesque."

Molly snorted. "Just you wait. She'll be wearin' football gear and tacklin' her brother before the year is out."

"Please, not that soon. Let them be sweet and tiny for a month or two at least," Eden prayed, then chuckled just as her stomach growled. "Okay, okay. I'll make it three muffins, but then I have to get back to work."

Molly clicked her tongue. "It'll be sooner than you think. Which is why you need to be taking care to save your strength instead of working so hard."

"Dr. Tremont says I'm doing great. I'm not working too hard at all. Just hard enough." No doubt self-employment came with many perks the fashion industry did not. A steady paycheck wasn't one of them, however. "Don't forget, I have a future to see to."

Piling muffins onto a fruit-patterned platter, Molly slanted Eden a pointed glance. "You ought to have a man taking care of the future."

Eden propped her hand at her hip. "Come on, Molly. Don't tell me you think I can't provide for my family without help from a man."

The slow shake of Molly's head covered volumes of old-world opinion on modern family values. "These babies' father has a lot to answer for."

Eden couldn't argue with that because Molly was right. Nate did have a lot to answer for—lying by omission being at the top of the list. Being a no-account scumbag summed up the rest. Cups rattled against saucers as Eden gathered both for tea.

Molly hovered nearby. "I wish you'd let me do that."

"Thanks, but I'm fine," Eden said, and meant it. The scumbag was history. Like Custer. Or Waterloo. The Great Depression. Black Monday.

The teakettle whistled, and she applied herself to the task at hand, pouring water over bags of spiced tea before setting the table with plates, knives and sweet cream butter.

Insisting that Molly join her for the last quiet minutes before the shop opened, Eden eased down into a chair and split open a steaming muffin. Eyes closed, she filled her head with the sweet scent of warm honey.

"Promise me one thing, Molly."

"What's that?" Molly asked, reaching for a muffin and a spoon of peach jam.

"If you and Tucker ever close Hansen's Heaven,

promise me you'll give me this recipe. I'm officially addicted to your muffins." Eden reached across the table to brush a crumb from Molly's collar.

"Close the bakery?" Molly asked, glancing down to make sure no crumbs remained on the front of her jumper. "Why would we close the bakery?"

"You don't have any plans to retire?"

"Retire?" Molly huffed. "And do what?"

Eden shrugged. "Nothing?"

This time Molly's response was a sharp frown.

"Okay. Then everything," Eden said and gestured expansively. "All the things you've wanted to do in your life but haven't managed to get to yet."

"And those would be?"

"Travel?"

"Nowhere I want to go."

"Truly?" Molly nodded, and Eden thought more. "Books you haven't yet read. A language you've wanted to learn. A class you've always been meaning to take."

"Eden," Molly began, drawing a patient breath, "I read a dozen romance novels a month. Speaking English suits me fine. I have seventy-two years' worth of learning stored up. If I take a class in anything, I won't be able to get a hat on my head."

Molly patted her close-cropped silver hair and Eden laughed. Then she realized she had a woman in front of her who had lived a full life. A woman who was also her friend.

"What's on your mind, Eden?"

Hmm. A friend she hadn't realized was psychic. Eden smiled and ran a fingertip around the scalloped edge of the muffin plate. "Do you ever wonder if you've missed out on anything? Or wish you'd done more with your life?"

"No." Molly didn't even hesitate. "My life's been filled with a husband and sons and friends as dear to me as family. If I've missed anything, so be it. If I'd've done more, I don't know where I would've put it."

Plain-spoken words of wisdom. Exactly what Eden had known Molly would say. Still, because she was in such a state of personal flux, she had to ask, "Then you're happy with the choices you've made? You don't have any regrets?"

"Regrets? If I thought it mattered, I suppose I could come up with one or two. But, yes, I'm happy. What good would it do me to be anything but?" Molly buttered and jammed her remaining muffin half. "Wonderin' and wishin' don't change what's gone before. Now, why do you ask?"

Eden shrugged. "No particular reason. Just wanted to make sure—"

"Don't worry about making sure." Molly squeezed Eden's hand with her own strong fingers. "Worry about making a life."

It was hard to wash down the last morsel of melt-in-your-mouth muffin with the lump that had risen in her throat. But Eden managed to do that, and to push away from the table without revealing any more of her turmoil than she could help.

Change would be a good thing. She needed to keep that in mind. "You feed me well, Molly, my dear, but if Ben or Beth gain another ounce, I won't be able to get into any of my clothes."

"You haven't gained an ounce to begin with. Nothing that isn't babies, anyway." Molly dragged out a chair and motioned for Eden to put up her feet. "Sit while I do up these dishes."

Eden offered but a token protest. She *was* strangely tired. "You're going to spoil me."

"It took two pregnancies, but Tucker convinced me that expectant mothers deserve to be spoiled. As I recall, he refused to take no for an answer." Molly sighed, the sound long and reminiscent. Then she shook off the daydream and scurried around until the kitchen shone spic-and-span.

After drying her hands, she picked up her basket and linked her arm through Eden's for the walk to the front of the store. "Do you need anything before I go?"

Still trying to picture the contradiction of tiny Tucker Hansen standing up to Molly, it took a minute for Eden's mind to switch gears. "As a matter of fact, yes. Do you know of anyone local who does carpentry work?"

"Something wrong with the house?"

"The house is perfect," Eden hurriedly assured her friend. "It's just that I'm running out of display room. I've been toying with the idea of having shelves built.

"I don't have enough room to hang everything, but with shelves I could stack the excess stock rather than keeping it stored in my sewing room. And my bedroom. And the nursery."

"Business boomin'?"

"Better than I could've imagined." Eden crossed the fingers of both hands. "I'm hoping the Spring Fest will be the icing on the cake. In less than five months, I'll have two more mouths to feed. I need to make a name for The Fig Leaf now."

Molly stared long and hard, then bit back what was no doubt another admonishment and said instead, "Jace Morgan."

"Excuse me?" Eden had been braced for an argument, not a name.

"Jace Morgan. He did most of the original renovations to this house." Molly's gaze circled the room. "Does the best work I've ever seen."

"He's local, then?"

Molly nodded. "Lives outside of town. Don't think I know anyone who's ever been out to his place."

Another man with secrets. Great. "How do I get in touch with him?"

Molly brushed aside the lace curtain covering the front door's etched window. "I saw his truck in front of The Emporium on my way over. I'll see if he's still there. If not, I'll find him." Letting the curtain fall back in place, Molly pulled open the door and sailed out with only a backward wave.

Watching Molly go, Eden wondered about Jace Morgan. Then, as the door eased shut, wondered what caliber gun it would take to blast the door-chime beyond recognition. Flipping the sign to OPEN, she returned to the sewing room.

The whir of the motor, the click of the footfeed and the snip of the scissors filled the quiet house.

Thirty minutes later, the chime sounded again. Eden shut down the machine, gathered up a sketch pad and pencil and headed into the shop.

She climbed onto the stool behind the L-shaped counter at the rear of the store and called, "Good morning," to the two ladies scanning the racks of baby clothes she'd ordered from a seamstress in Miami with a wicked needle and a love of the islands.

Fifteen minutes later, three young women maneuvered through the door and jostled packages across the shop to a selection of one-of-a-kind drop-waisted sarongs and matching midriff-baring tops. Taking in the customers' collective excitement, Eden couldn't help but smile. Wouldn't Wynnella die to see this whispered enthusiasm over her work.

Eden knew her collection was unconventional by Texas Hill Country standards. Yet even before she'd begun her career, her fashion instincts had been right on. Women were women, no matter the place they called home. Quality clothing, even when out of the ordinary and a tad offbeat, was always welcomed by dressers of discriminating taste.

The first two shoppers approached the counter. "This dress is lovely," remarked the taller of the women. She handed Eden a dainty christening gown. "Do you do the needlework yourself?"

"Oh, no. This designer is Cuban and the mother of twelve. And she's been able to put at least three of those children through college on my purchases alone." The woman and her companion both laughed while Eden smoothed and folded the gown. "Let me guess; a new grandchild in the family?"

"My very first." Pulling a picture from her wallet, she offered it to Eden.

Babies. Eden couldn't think of anything in the world more precious. Anything that brought more joy, more fulfillment. More hope for the future. So, why did she feel such trepidation when she knew the changes she'd made in her life were in her children's best interest?

Because you're not sure they're in yours? Eden pushed aside the thought and returned the photo. "An excellent choice. She'll look positively angelic in white."

"My dear, she looks positively angelic in anything!" The woman laughed. "Your selection of baby things is absolutely to die for. I feel a spending frenzy coming on."

"Any time you're struck with an uncontrollable urge, please stop by." Eden rang up the sale and handed the woman her business card.

When the chime rang out again, she caught a glimpse of a man in black before turning back to her customers. "I'm sure I can find the perfect something for your granddaughter. Remember, Wynnella still has nine educations to finance."

"I have a feeling the next three degrees will be on me," the woman admitted, taking the package from Eden. "I'll be seeing you again soon."

"I'll look forward to it," Eden replied.

The door closed behind them and Eden glanced toward the three women modeling the sarongs for one another. Knowing friendly competition often decided a sale, she declined offering unneeded help. Settling her glasses on the end of her nose, she picked up her pencil, then turned her attention to the man.

He stood in front of the bay window, a dark silhouette on lace curtains of white. Jet black hair brushed his forehead and nape; the windblown locks framed a strong, square jaw. His shoulders were dangerously wide, his waist trim, his wide-legged stance cocky—and marginally suggestive, Eden mused, noticing too well the fit of his jeans.

He needed a shave. Or would have, had the dark shadow been worn for style. As it was, the stubble fit the image of a man comfortable in his own skin. No, more than comfortable: confident. Certain. His bold self-assurance hovered just this side of arrogance.

An interesting evaluation, because Eden knew without a doubt that he had no idea of the impression he made. His cocky air fit him as naturally as the rest of his muscled body. In fact, he seemed totally unaware of the interested glances the young female shoppers tossed his way.

His interest, instead, lay in a wisp of a baby blanket woven with threads of delicate white and shot with strands of silver and gold. He rubbed one palm over the fabric, then stroked the cloth between his forefinger and thumb. Eden caught her breath at the incongruous picture: the ethereal blanket held in the hands of an earthy man.

Fingers of sunlight winnowed through the lace covered window at his side, catching strands of blue in the black of his hair. The muted beams brushed

his face, highlighting his cheekbones and his renegade's mouth. When the thick fringe of lashes lifted
slowly, Eden found herself looking into a pair of pale
blue eyes.

She'd known attractive men in her previous life,
had worked with several during her years at *Elite
Woman* Magazine. But none of them had possessed
more than a degree of this man's I-have-what-you-
need sensuality. This man's man. No, she amended
privately—this woman's man.

Enchanted, Eden started to smile. Before she
could manage, though, he'd turned, replacing the
blanket on the shelf. He wandered the store's pe-
rimeter, studying the molded cornice and the sten-
ciled frieze. He seemed to be admiring the work, or
passing judgment. Eden couldn't decide which.

She released the breath held tight in her lungs
and watched his progress over the rim of her glasses.
At least she watched until one of the women brought
her selection to the counter.

"Will that be all?" Eden asked, annoyed to find
that she had to force her mind back to business
when business, not a man, should've been all she
had on her mind.

"It's not all I'd like to have, but it seems to be all
I'll be leaving with," the woman answered, leveling
a sultry look over her shoulder at the devil who
hadn't once glanced in her direction.

Eden smiled at the woman making the purchase,
smiled even more broadly at the woman's presump-
tion. It was an evil thing to even consider, but . . .

the very devil in question made her do it. She leaned forward and whispered, "He must be gay."

"Think so?" The woman raised her chin, as if Eden's remark had stroked her neck rather than her ego. She cast another glance over her shoulder and swung her shopping bag onto her arm. "Well, Mr. Tall-Dark-and-Sexy doesn't know what he's missing," she said, and followed her friends out the door.

Oh, somehow I think he does, Eden thought, her gaze returning again to the man. He *was* sexy. And if he was gay, well . . . that wasn't going to stop her from enjoying the show as he approached the counter.

Stalked more aptly described his leggy stride. Long, lithe, and superbly lean, he moved with a predator's agile grace, not a move wasted as his moccasins whisked across the hardwood floor.

Threadbare jeans, worn out honestly, fit his thighs like nobody's business. A black T-shirt, equally thin in the points of most wear, hugged his torso. A most impressive torso, Eden noted, now that he stood but two feet away.

She clasped her hands together on the counter. "Can I help you select something? A baby gift, perhaps?"

"No, thanks. I don't need a baby gift."

Hmm. Strike one. "Something for your wife, then?"

"Nope. No wife, either."

O . . . kay. She'd try a different tack. "Fine. Is there anything I can do for you?"

"You can tell me if you're Eden Karr."

Eden nodded. "I am. And you are . . . ?"

"Jace Morgan." He produced another oh-so-breathtaking smile. "Molly sent me over. Shelves, I think she said."

"Well, you're certainly a surprise." Eden extended a hand over the counter. Jace's palm was hard and callused; his handshake firm, strong, stable. She hated pulling away.

"A surprise in what way?" he finally asked.

After Molly's brief description, she'd expected a reclusive old geezer. Not a cross between savage and seraph. She wasn't about to tell him that, however. What she did tell him was, "I don't know. I expected someone who looked like a carpenter."

Jace scratched his whiskered jaw; his palm covered most of that sexy smile. "What exactly does a carpenter look like?"

Eden propped her chin in her fist and pretended to give the question serious thought. "Maybe more sweat and sawdust. Nails clenched between your teeth. A ladder hung over your shoulder. And"—she gestured with one hand—"wearing those pants with hammers and tape measures hung everywhere."

Jace's laugh was a low-throated growl. "The sweat's a job away. So's the sawdust. The ladder's in the truck. And the tools . . ." He patted his pockets, front and rear, finally coming up with a single nail. He balanced it head down on the counter. "Will that do?"

Eden's gaze traveled from his pockets to the nail to his face. She felt a shiver start bone deep. "Is that your résumé?"

"No, ma'am." He glanced around the room, the pride of a creator in his eyes. "This is my résumé."

Her gaze followed his. "Then you're hired."

He slowly turned back to face her, one brow lifted. "Just like that? No references? No Better Business Bureau report?"

"Molly Hansen is all the reference I need."

Pacing an aisle, Jace stopped and fingered a brightly woven shawl. "Like the man said, 'I may not be cheap, but I can be had.' "

"Quality is never cheap." And if he could be had . . . She wouldn't think about that. "I don't mind the cost, as long as I get what I pay for."

"You'll get it." Jace studied the floor between his feet for a second before his gaze fastened on hers. "But I won't sign a contract under any terms but my own. Even if it means no deal. What I do takes time. I don't have a problem with deadlines, unless it means my work will suffer."

Eden wondered how this man's work could ever suffer. His arrogance—and by now she'd decided it was exactly that—was that of a consummate artist. And that very same arrogance convinced her that he was the man for the job. She'd seen the sparkle in his eyes as he surveyed his craftsmanship.

"What exactly are your terms?"

"I supply materials at cost. But it's the only break you get." Strolling from one side of the store to the other, he examined the existing shelf space with a critical eye. "What time do you close?"

"Five o'clock. Why?"

"I'll be back then." He started for the door and

added, "With tape measure in hand. You can show me exactly what you have in mind and I'll work up an estimate."

"Fine." Laying her glasses on the register, Eden eased off the stool and skirted the counter just as Jace stepped out the front door. He ran his hand over the gingerbread cornice tucked into the corner of the covered porch, frowning when he noticed a chip in the wood.

Oh yes, this man was exactly what she needed. "I'll see you around five, then."

He turned, stopping midstep. The hand he offered froze, then dropped to his side.

Eden glanced up. An undefined emotion flashed through his eyes—eyes focused on her stomach. She took a protective step in retreat, wrapped her arms over her middle, and held her breath.

His gaze crawled over the bulge of her belly to her face. "Hell, woman. You're pregnant."

TWO

Oh, boy.

Tension ebbed between them, as thick as road tar. As thick as Molly Hansen's peach jam. As thick as Eden's waistline.

She took a retreating, slow-motion step. The defensive move lifted her off the sidewalk, into the doorway of the store and put her at eye level with Jace. She took full advantage.

"Yes. I am." Her mouth drew tight. "Is that a problem?"

Jace cut her off with a quick shake of his head. He scrubbed a hand through his hair, then let the locks fall, his black brows two slashes of indecision, or confusion, or both.

"It's not a problem. Just a . . . surprise. I'll see you this evening." Backing down the walk, he finally produced a hint of his devil's smile. And then he was gone.

Eden stepped into the safety of the shop, closed the door and leaned back. Dizziness swirled behind her eyes in multicolored hues. Blood pounded in her hands and feet. Breathing seemed more effort than it was worth.

Okay. He'd made a comment. What he'd said was nothing to get worked up over, especially when Jace Morgan was a stranger whose opinion of her condition meant nothing in the grand scheme of things.

Not like the opinion that had mattered most and had crushed her like a bug beneath a shoe. Nate Armstrong had made her an offer—a monetary settlement in exchange for her silence in the matter of her children's paternity.

"Think about it, Eden," the Manhattan attorney had argued, after confessing that he'd been married for the past eleven years. "If this gets out, I'll be ruined."

"Sounds like a personal problem to me," she'd replied, holding on to enough pride to keep her voice even, her chin high.

The rest of her pride she'd had to work to rebuild; not an easy feat after her blindly stupid error in judgment. How could an educated, savvy, nineties' woman be so naive? If she could pull that rabbit out of her hat, maybe she'd better understand how she'd been duped by Nate's illusion.

After three years of stolen weekends and romantic getaways and enough of his things left at her place that he never went home when she was in town, Eden had thought she and Nate had a future.

She supposed he had loved her in his own twisted way. But Nate Armstrong's twisted *love* she'd had no trouble leaving behind. Other things were not so cut and dried.

Painted white and trimmed in midnight blue, the gabled house she now called home was a far cry from the Soho loft she'd shared with Nate on the days and nights she'd spent in New York between the stories that sent her out on the road.

Now, instead of a sunken Jacuzzi, she soaked away the stress of the day in a clawfoot tub. When she tumbled out of bed each morning, her feet met hardwood floor rather than Oriental rug. Her kitchen was no longer state-of-the-art, but a functional work of art; her antiques more serviceable than valuable.

Turning her back on editorial meetings, temperamental models, last-minute rescheduling of stories and photo spreads—not to mention the man who'd rejected her marriage proposal because he'd been married to another—she'd been driven to her new life by memories of the past, of growing up in a close-knit, loving household.

The life she'd lived in the early years, before she'd succumbed to the lure of the Paris runways, was exactly the life she wished to give her children. And she couldn't provide that carefree existence when she lived in a whirlwind of spur-of-the-moment travel and seventy-hour work weeks.

Returning to her roots seemed the obvious place to begin her quest. She'd grown up in Dallas, in a family who believed wholeheartedly in summer vacations. She'd first seen Arbor Glen when she was but fourteen. And she'd been touched, even at that young age, by the wholesomeness of the town. Dorky for a kid to think that, she knew, but the contrast

from her urban home had struck a lingering chord.
And she'd wondered what it must be like to live in
such serenity. She'd yet to find that, or true peace
of mind. Or a sign that the choices she made were
right . . . or wise. After all, the decision had been
one made in a hurry, much like the whirlwind beginning of her relationship with Nate—and look
what that lack of exercised judgment had wrought.

She hoped that confidence and personal fulfillment would come. With time. With patience. And
with a little help from her friends.

With a deep, cleansing breath, Eden pushed away
from the door and headed back to the counter. Before she made it all the way, the doorchime tolled.
Hands full, Chloe Angelino burst into the shop,
bumping the door shut with one hip.

"Hello, Chloe," Eden said as the girl fairly floated
across the room.

Chloe's peasant skirt of lemon-colored gauze hovered inches over her bare toes. Tendrils of blond
hair rebelled at her topknot and hung in wisps
around her gamine face. Brown doe eyes, at odds
with her aura of light, added to her other-worldly
presence.

Only her half-laced camisole gave a clue to the
budding woman disguised as a waif of sixteen.

Eden rounded the counter just as Chloe dropped
a half ream of colored papers next to the register.
White dust rose in puffs around the stack.

The teen frowned and glanced at her chalky
hands. "Guess I should have come here straight

from the print shop instead of stopping by the studio."

"No problem. What's a little chalk dust between friends?" Eden waved her hand to clear the air.

"I knew you'd understand." Chloe leaned forward, pressed a chalky palm to her heart. The silver bells between her breasts tinkled. "This morning in history we studied the Trail of Tears. I saw a wise and ancient Cherokee squaw. She called to the blood of her people flowing in my soul, so I had to stop by the studio and sketch her."

Eden looked the girl square in the eye. "You're Greek, Chloe. Not Cherokee."

Chloe straightened. "My father, Nicholas, is Greek. I am of the earth." She spun a circle where she stood, then propped both elbows on the counter and released a gust of breath. "Anyway, yours was my last delivery."

Eden picked a sheet off the stack. "So, what is it exactly that you've brought me?"

"Freedom Advertising printed flyers for the Spring Fest. It's my design, you know."

"No. I didn't." But now that she looked closely, Eden saw a bit of Chloe's whimsy in the ad. "You did a great job."

Chloe eyed the paper, then skirted the counter and sidled closer to Eden. She stared at her fingernails when she spoke. "Can I talk to you a sec?"

Eden looked from the paper to the girl. "Sure, honey. What's wrong?"

"It's my dad." Chloe shifted from one foot to the other, gestured with her hands. "He's like . . . sick."

"Has he gone to the doctor?"

She shook her head, straw-colored wisps of hair catching on her lashes. "Not that kind of sick. He's not running a fever or anything. He just doesn't talk. He stays in the shop and works all the time. He won't come home. He never sleeps."

This wasn't like Nick Angelino at all. Eden knew he'd recently lost his wife, but he'd remained an attentive father. Or so it had appeared.

Eden tempered her worry with a gentle smile. "Chloe, your dad gets involved with his work. When he's intent on a sculpture or a painting, he barely comes up for air for two or three days."

Chloe's eyes grew wide, and her mouth quivered. "It's not like that. I'm afraid he's gonna get real bad again. Like . . . when my mom died."

"Tell you what," Eden began, swallowing hard, uncertain she was equipped to offer what Chloe needed. "I'm fixing a pot of shrimp Creole tonight. Why don't you come by around six-thirty and I'll send some home for you and your dad?" She thought a moment more, then smiled. "He won't be able to say no if you tell him Eden said he needed to eat."

Chloe nodded, tears glimmering in her tawny eyes. She sniffed, rubbed her palm over her nose. Then the troubled teen transformed into the town's fey sprite. She thrust her chin in the air. "I must go."

"Not so fast," Eden ordered as Chloe quickly donned her mask. "I want to talk to you about working for me."

"I work for Nicholas. I work for Freedom Adverthing. I have no more time." She took a step toward the door.

"This wouldn't be full-time. Just a special project. An art project." Eden aligned the flyers and scooted them next to her register. "I'm sure your father wouldn't mind."

"I must go." Chloe's sigh was huge and theatrical. She regarded the glare Eden threw over the rims of her glasses. "But I will appear at dusk," she added, disappearing out the door in a tangle of yellow gauze and silver chains.

Eden watched the girl go, feeling a reverse sense of déjà vu. Sixteen years from now, Bethany would be that age. Between now and then, Eden was going to have to figure out this mothering thing.

Food was a comfort, but not a long-term solution. And the distraction of work only lasted until the project was complete. How well Eden knew the latter.

Chloe's dramatic personality was a costume, her theatrics a prop she used to keep others at a distance. Eden recognized the ruse.

Since leaving New York, she'd done much the same thing. Molly had been the first new friend to find a place in Eden's heart. And then had come Chloe.

Eden wasn't as blindly trusting of people as she'd been before Nate. Especially now that she had two other lives to consider. But she and Chloe had both been hurt, each in their own way. Perhaps they'd been thrown together to be healed.

* * *

At a quarter to five that evening, Jace guided his truck down the rutted drive connecting his property to Highway 37. As he made the turn onto the black-top strip that led to Arbor Glen, he tried to figure out which one of his big feet he'd stuck in his big mouth this afternoon in front of Eden Karr.

She was a pregnant customer. A pregnant *paying* customer. It wasn't like he had anything against expectant women. Hey, if his mother hadn't gotten pregnant, where would he be today?

But seeing a woman in Eden's condition tended to remind him of Kevin Nelson, the first of the "Four to Score" to drop out of The Race.

The Race had been a competition born after a Spring Break keg party during the Four's senior year at Texas A & M. Jace, Kevin, Robert Scott and Jimmy "The Marv" Marvin had chased one another's accomplishments since they'd hooked up in junior high.

The Race just put a formal, and admittedly ferocious, spin on a rivalry that had spanned half their lifetimes.

Kevin had married months after graduation. He and Terri tried for years to start a family. When Terri finally became pregnant, Kevin swore nothing would keep him from being there for his kid. He was through with twelve- to fourteen-hour days and left a career in aeronautics to teach calculus at a high school in Terri's Colorado hometown.

Even cutting short a day of Saturday meetings, Jace had only managed to make it to the last hour of the going away barbecue he and Robert and Marv had thrown.

Some friend he'd been, Jace thought, slowing his truck as the speed limit changed. Too bad his grand epiphany hadn't happened three years sooner. He might not have lost touch with his best friends if it had.

He wondered how Kevin, Terri and the kid were doing now. Yeah, he still had a few regrets that he hadn't flown up to Colorado for a visit after the baby'd been born—*way* after the baby'd been born, of course.

After pacing the stain off the floor while his Alaskan malamute, Chelsea, had given birth six weeks ago, Jace doubted he'd have survived waiting out Terri's labor—though a true friend would've been there for Kev and at least made the effort.

Jace hadn't. And the baby had to be at least three by now.

With the sun warming the back of his neck, Jace pulled his pickup to a stop in front of The Fig Leaf. A funny knot coiled in the pit of his stomach.

He rubbed the lump with the heel of his hand, wondering why, after all these years, his past had intruded on the present, reminding him painfully that he had a lot to make up for. Not to mention a woman he needed to keep at a distance, keep from becoming friendly with, since he had such a crummy track record of being there for friends.

"Yeah, yeah, yeah," he muttered under his breath, climbing from the cab to jerk his toolbox from the bed of the truck. "Who says she wants to be friends with you anyway."

His workboots clomped against the plank sidewalk fronting the stores. The sign in Eden's window said CLOSED, but he tried the door anyway and found it open.

He set his toolbox inside. "Eden?"

"Back here."

Her muffled voice reached his ears at the same time the smells hit his nose. Nostrils flared, he inhaled the spicy combination of garlic, onion, tomato and green pepper. An apology of sorts formed on his tongue as he made his way through the connecting rooms of the house.

Molly hadn't told him that Eden was pregnant. She'd told him Eden was a single woman living alone, then gone on to ask his help as a personal favor. He was a sap for Molly Hansen. How could he say no?

Besides, he'd never turned down the chance to play Prince Charming for a damsel in distress.

This damsel just happened to be a hell of a gorgeous woman. Green eyes that saw everything but pretended not to. Lips as cool and sleek as a polished cherry. A nose that might've had a superior tilt if not for that barely noticeable crook to the left.

But gorgeous or not, unless he was *way* off the mark here, she belonged to someone else. At least she had belonged. Very recently, in fact. Which brought up a lot of questions Jace wasn't sure he wanted to ask. Or to have answered.

He stopped at the kitchen door, all his preconceived notions about pregnant women shot to the moon. Not that he'd ever put a name to what those notions were. But he knew he'd never used the word *pregnant* in the same sentence as *sexy*.

His gut clenched. Hard.

Eden stood on a chair, her backside at eye level. Rifling through a cabinet, she picked up one jar, set it down, picked up another. Hair the color of burnished mahogany bounced on her shoulders as she moved.

His gaze swept lower, taking in the fullness of one breast, the bare swell of her belly, the seat of her outfit draped intimately across her bottom. All the while her hips swayed and she hummed along with the radio blaring from the top of the refrigerator.

"Hi." She turned, caught him staring, bit off the word. Indignation sparked in her eyes.

He met her gaze, knowing he deserved the wrath of a woman scorned. And then he realized she was standing on a chair. He might not know a lot about pregnant women, but he was sure she had no business standing on a chair.

"Uh, should you be up there like that?"

"You know," she began, paying no attention to his question, "this is my only complaint about the whole house." She propped one fist on her hip and gestured with the spice jar still in her hand. "Two cabinets that stretch to the ceiling. Why not have four cabinets half the size?"

Amazing. He'd been fighting to form the apology of his life and she was running off at the mouth about cabinets. "The previous owner never could decide what to do in here."

"Well, when you're through with the shop, maybe we can talk about this mess."

"Then I'm not fired?"

Tossing him the spice jar, she eased down to sit on the edge of the counter, leaving her feet in the chair. A frown drew her brows together. "Why would I fire you? Wait. I know. You lied to me on your résumé."

Jace set the jar on the table and fought back a grin. "No. But I wasn't exactly Prince Charming this afternoon."

Gripping the edges of the counter at her sides, Eden cocked her head to the side. "Ah, but I am learning that frogs have a variety of uses."

"Ribbit," Jace croaked, and Eden laughed. Crossing the room, he stopped and braced his palms on the back of her chair. Less than a foot of free space separated them. And that was much too close. "Do you need help getting down?"

Delicious humor sparkled in eyes greener than a stalk of spring grass. "Sure. Why not?"

Great. Now what was he supposed to do?

"Jace?"

"Hmm . . . oh, here." Shoving the chair to the side, he cupped her near elbow with his hand and stretched out his other arm as a lever. She scooted her seat toward the edge of the counter. Each move pressed her belly against his wrist. A bead of sweat rolled down his temple. "Wait, let me—"

"No. This is fine." Using his shoulder for support,

she maneuvered off the edge on her own, stepped back and looked him up one side and down the other. "This is your first pregnancy, isn't it?"

"Why do you say that?"

"You act like I'll give birth here on the kitchen floor if you touch me, and I don't plan on going into labor for about five more months. Trust me. I'm tougher than I look."

"I hope so," he murmured beneath his breath.

"Men." She gave a dismissive sniff and crossed the blue-and-white-tiled floor to the stove. Picking up a wooden spoon and the spice jar, she sprinkled pepper into the cast-iron pot, then stirred the bubbling contents. The pungent aroma of Creole cooking drifted across the room. Jace's stomach growled.

Eden chuckled, peered into the pot and pronounced the mixture, "Perfect. Have you eaten?"

Jace leaned against the pie safe next to the stove. He stuffed his fingers into the front pockets of his jeans. "Not since this morning."

Pulling down bowls from cabinet number two, she said, "Well, you're welcome to join me. We're having shrimp Creole. And rolls Molly brought by this afternoon."

"Mmm. Molly's rolls. I'll take a dozen," he answered, realizing Eden's company appealed to him as much as the food.

Grinning, Eden turned away to set bowls, spoons, saucer, and hot mats on the table. She grabbed a pot of rice, placed it on the table, then reached for the kettle of Creole.

He beat her to it. "I'll get it."

"Thanks," she said and slowly eased her body into a chair. "There's a pitcher of milk in the fridge."

"Milk?" Smiling, Jace reached behind him and opened the refrigerator.

"For us motherly types," Eden teased. "I think there's a bottle of wine in the back. Or there might be a beer. Tucker leaves one here occasionally."

He found the beer behind fresh fruits and vegetables and enough yogurt to stock a small grocery. He set the pitcher of milk on the table, then screwed the cap from the beer bottle and raised it to his lips.

"Oh. The rolls." Eden moved to scoot back.

Jace grabbed the seat of her chair. His hand brushed her leg; her long, well-shaped leg. He left it there, feeling soft female skin covered by thin cotton. He wanted to feel more. He was feeling too much already. "I'll get them."

Eden only nodded and handed him a pot holder.

The heat from the oven blasted his face and took his mind off another warmth he had no business feeling. This was a business dinner, nothing more. Brushing her leg had been an accident. It meant nothing more than shaking her hand this afternoon. Or the way his arm grazed her stomach minutes ago.

Innocent touches, he told himself. Simple. Unplanned. That was all, he argued; then he argued more. Unplanned, sure, that he could buy.

But there was nothing simple about the very complicated knot into which his feelings were tied. Especially since there was still a big piece missing from this picture.

What had happened to the man in her life? Not

that he cared. He didn't. Nope. Not a bit. Because this job would be a whole lot simpler if caring stayed out of the way.

Eden ladled out two huge bowls of shrimp Creole over rice and Jace turned his concentration to the simple pleasure of a home-cooked dinner. Eden seemed hungry as well. Not a word passed between them, the only sound that of flatware on crockery, the ticking clock, a slow dripping faucet. As Jace buttered his third roll, he glanced up to find a smile on Eden's lips.

"What?" He mouthed the word around the warm, yeasty bread.

"You look like you might make that dozen after all."

He nodded toward her empty bowl. "You didn't do too badly either."

Patting her firm stomach, Eden shoved away from the table. "I have a good excuse. I'm eating for more than one."

With the top she was wearing it was hard to tell. Jace dusted the bread crumbs over his saucer. "This was great. Do you cook like this all the time?"

She lifted one shoulder. "I cook all the time, if that's what you mean."

"What I mean is that it's a lot of work to go to for just one person."

"True. But I'm worth it. And . . . I love it," she said, seeming surprised. "Besides, I don't do such a bad job, if I do say so myself."

He nodded toward the empty bowls on the table. "You do a damn fine job."

"Thanks. I probably should've taken time to discover that before now. I've never had a lot of opportunity to cook." She frowned and pressed her fist to her sternum. "Though Creole might not have been the best choice."

"Why's that?"

"It's giving me heartburn already." She grimaced. "I can't imagine what the spices will do to my milk."

Jace wasn't touching that one. Uh-uh. No way. He twirled his empty longneck on the table.

Eden glanced up. Her eyes widened with an awareness of what she'd just said. And who she'd said it to. "Oops. I guess *that* just took away the rest of your appetite."

God, she really had great eyes, Jace thought, watching the twinkle of green brighten as she smiled. He patted his stomach, as if checking his appetite. "Yep. It's history. But you can blame that on the food," he added when her smile threatened to fade, "not the conversation."

Her hair glittered under the light when she cocked her head to one side. "Flattery will get you everywhere, you know."

Business, Morgan. Keep it business. He glanced around the room. "I'm hoping it will get me a shot at this kitchen."

"Between the flattery and your résumé, I'd say the job's yours." Eden pushed her saucer away and settled back with a keen eye. "But it's not the priority the shop is."

"I know. And I couldn't get to it for a while anyway.

You know The Glen? The Bed and Breakfast out on 37?"

"Belongs to the Browns, right?" Her expression changed the minute the light dawned. "You're doing the renovations?"

Jace nodded. "That's *my* priority right now."

Eden frowned. "You think you'll have time to do this job on the side?"

"Not a problem. I'm waiting on a back order." He shrugged. "The nature of the business."

"Funny. I was just weighing the supposed perks of self-employment earlier myself."

"I'll wait on a dozen back orders before I'll ever wait in Stemmons Freeway traffic again. The pace of life in Arbor Glen beats the pants off the dance I did the years I lived in Dallas."

"I thought Molly said you were local."

"Three years local, but not born and bred."

"Then you're from Dallas?"

"Been there most of my life. But for a four-year stint in College Station. Texas A & M."

"And here I thought you were just a good ol' country boy."

"That's exactly what I am. Now, anyway. Had to work the rat race outta my system first. Those corporate ladders are hell on a country boy's vertigo."

"I had a place in New York until three months ago." She released a heavy sigh. Her belly lifted with the effort. "I don't miss everything about the city—but I can't say I'll never go back."

"Oh, I can say that in at least ten languages. You

couldn't pay me enough to get me back into a shirt and tie."

Scraping back her chair, Eden stood to stack his bowl and spoon in hers. "You don't believe clothes make the man?"

"Make him insane, maybe." Jace glanced around the kitchen. She was right. The cabinets really needed to go. "I kinda like sitting at my drafting table in boxers or briefs."

Eden cleared her throat, which brought Jace's head back around. What had he just said? Oh, yeah. He grinned. "Appetites don't stand a chance around here, do they?"

She rolled her eyes while gathering the saucers and remaining flatware. She carried the dishes to the sink, then turned back to face him. "You want to take a look at the shop now?"

"Sure." Back to business. That's what he needed. Sitting in *her* kitchen eating *her* food talking about *his* boxers and *her* milk . . . He blew out a long breath and followed her to the front of the store. "What did you have in mind?"

She walked between the hanging racks, fingering one garment after another. "You must know the Spring Fest is in three weeks."

"Yeah. Molly volunteered me for the committee running the electric for the dance."

"That sounds like the Molly I know."

"She does have a knack for getting her way."

"You've noticed?"

He stopped, held out both hands. "I'm here, aren't I?"

Her laugh tickled his ears. "My biggest problem lies in lack of space, both display and storage. What I'd like to do is build shelving along this back wall, then hang sample items on a rack."

"How tall do you need the rack?" Jace asked, thinking of the merchandise in his barn.

"At least eye level. That will give customers a clear view of what they want, plus keep the full-length items from dragging the ground."

Jace took measurements where necessary and jotted down notes and figures. He listened to Eden with only one ear, running a mental inventory of the supplies he'd need. Finally, he looked up from the tablet to find her steady gaze regarding him with mild amusement.

"How long have I been gone?" he asked.

"Five minutes or so."

The light fixture behind her lit the fire in her hair. The one directly above flickered over the freckles dusting her creamy complexion. He smelled peaches. No, apricots. He took a step away.

"I tend to do that. Get wrapped up in my work, that is." His voice sounded strained. As excuses went this one was lousy, but better than giving his imagination license to envision copper-colored specks on sun-kissed skin.

"I need someone who'll do a good job. Getting wrapped up in your work makes me think you might be the someone I'm looking for." Eden pushed her fists against her arched back. "Why don't you go ahead and do what you need to do in here to finish the estimate? I need to get back and clean up the kitchen."

"Sure. It won't take me long." He stuck his pencil behind his ear and watched Eden walk away. At least he watched her until she turned around and caught him at it.

Then he got busy and measured the wall. Twice. The first time he had the tape upside down, because Eden's departing laugh rocked through him like nothing had in a very long time.

He'd never thought of a pregnant woman as sexy before. Hell, he'd never thought much about pregnancy at all. He'd been too busy jumping from the final rung of one ladder to the first of the next, making his climb to the top of the top of the top. He hadn't even stopped to think about his own mortality.

He hadn't thought about much beyond leaving his professional mark on the world. He hadn't thought about having a child at all. He jotted down some figures and rewound his tape. Maybe that was why he'd avoided Kevin and Terri and the baby. Kevin had accomplished what Jace hadn't.

Jace grinned to himself. He really needed to go see the bum. He needed to find Robert and Marv; see how those two were doing. He needed to do a lot of things, make a lot of amends—"Sh . . . oot. What're you doing here?"

Chloe Angelino stared at him from the other side of the room. His glance took in the closed door and her pleasure in his surprise at the same time.

"I came for dinner."

Hmm. That wasn't exactly what he'd meant. "I mean, how'd you get in?"

"Eden hates that chime. I make sure she doesn't have to hear it."

"Handy talent. You do a lot of breaking and entering?" She was obviously expected, so that wasn't what had happened here, but he'd heard more than one rumor about this girl being one sandwich short of a picnic.

"I did not break and enter."

"I know. That was a joke." When she didn't say anything else, he sighed. "Eden's in the kitchen."

She stayed where she was and studied the tools in his box. "Are you working for her?"

"Yeah."

She slanted him a wary glance. "A special project?"

"She needs some carpentry work done."

She only nodded, then began a wide circle of the room. "What carpentry work does she want you to do?"

Jace tossed the tape measure in his toolbox and propped his hands at his hips. "Shelves. On these walls."

"Yes. That would work."

Jace rolled his eyes and inwardly groaned. *Everyone's a critic.*

Chloe walked toward him then, her hands twisted together at her waist. The bones in her wrists were no bigger than pebbles, her fingers and arms supple like spring saplings. Yet her fingernails were chewed to the quick. And the dramatic circles under her eyes would never come off with soap and water.

She was nothing like he remembered his sister looking at that age. She'd been all-American, scrubbed clean, wrapped in ribbons and lace. This girl was haunted, a being from another place, another time. Her eyes met his, those two huge orbs of henna brown peering at him and seeing too much. Knowing more about him than he did . . .

Eden broke the moment, entering the room with a small crate in her hands. Jace stepped forward and took it from her. Her gaze was searching as it fed between him and Chloe. He gave Eden a quick nod, indicating what, he didn't know, because he didn't know what she was asking.

Seeming relieved, she turned a huge smile on Chloe. "Did you tell your father you were bringing him something to eat?"

"He's waiting at the kitchen table. I even tucked a napkin into his shirt."

"Good." Eden laced her fingers together. "Things will work out, Chloe. Just hang in there."

Chloe took the crate from Jace. Their hands brushed briefly. She gave him a serene, all-knowing nod.

He hurried to the front of the room. "Let me get the door for you."

"In a moment." Chloe set the crate on the floor, pulled Eden close and settled a kiss on her cheek.

"Thank you," Chloe said, then lifted her burden and carried it to the door.

When she reached Jace, she stopped and pointedly made eye contact. "Eden likes you. So I like you, too."

"Thanks, I think."

"You're welcome, I know," she replied, and stepped into the night.

Jace closed the door behind her and turned to Eden. "What was that?"

"*That* . . . was a teenager."

He shuddered. "Strange creature."

Eden crossed her arms over her chest. "They have their moments. Not unlike . . . frogs."

Jace looked at her then. Truly looked at her. At her mahogany hair and freckles, at her skin like cream that smelled of apricots, at her smile and sense of humor—the latter which he couldn't see but still . . . saw.

Suddenly, he needed breathing room in a big way. "Do you want to ride out to my shop?"

"Tonight?" She looked as surprised as he felt.

"Yeah. I've got a rack you might want to use in that corner. If you give me the okay, I can bring it out first thing in the morning."

"Sounds great."

"Then let's go," he said, knowing he needed to get this job done and get out of her life before the attraction grew into something he'd want to take further.

And with his track record for letting people down, it would be best if he didn't take it anywhere at all.

THREE

He lived in a barn. A real barn. A worn, weathered building that had once been home to animals, not some avant-garde designer's idea of fashionable back-to-basics, complete with modern amenities.

With nothing but a sliver of moon and a sprinkling of stars for light, Eden peered through the truck's windshield and decided Jace had no amenities.

He parked his truck under an aluminum awning. Sawhorses piled high with sheets of wood edged one side. Cases of wood finish and linseed oil lined the other. Eden could barely open her door. If she'd been any more pregnant, she wouldn't have been able to squeeze out of the cab.

"You need some help?"

"No, I've got it," she said. "It's just logistics. The round-peg-in-the-square-hole scenario."

Jace made no comment, but waited for her at the corner of the open structure. "I never think about the clutter out here. I'm the only one who ever sees it."

She dusted a cobweb from her sleeve. "Don't apologize."

"I didn't," Jace replied matter-of-factly. He led the

way down a short dirt track to the barn and, once there, lifted the four-by-eight beam slanted across the two doors.

"You leave your place unlocked?"

He pitched her a quizzical glance. "Don't you?"

That was one of the things that had taken getting used to. But she did. And she nodded. "Being out this far, though, I thought you'd be worried about vandals."

"Anyone who finds me is welcome to share what I have. Besides"—he shoved open one door and gave her that devil's grin—"I have a security system."

Two sharp whistles pierced the air. Seconds later, Eden found herself confronted with a thick ruff of silver fur and fangs. Jace stepped aside to let her go first. With her best are-you-out-of-your-mind scowl, she shook her head. The dog looked more like a wolf. Especially when he snarled.

"Chelsea, this is Eden. Eden, my Alaskan security system."

Eden tucked her hands in the pockets of her tunic and cocked one eyebrow. Jace was really working hard to fight back a grin.

"You two have something in common," Jace said.

Eden watched Chelsea trot out into the night. "What's that? Neither one of us has a waistline?"

"C'mon. I'll show you." He gestured for her to follow.

Jace closed the door, hit a switch and illuminated one long half of the temperature-controlled interior of the barn. Lathes, saws, drills, drafting boards and worktables made her forget she was anywhere but in the most modern of woodshops.

Eden made her way to where Jace waited expectantly at the opposite end of the building. She passed a spindle-back rocking chair and set it in motion, lingered in front of a pine armoire that was literally a work of art. Her steps slowed, but her mind raced. "You don't have a shop in Arbor Glen, do you?"

He shook his head. "I do the larger pieces on commission. I get most of my referrals from a display I have at a shop in Farmersville."

Her eyes widened. "The Old Pine Box?"

"Yeah."

"You're *the* mysterious J. B. Morgan?"

"Only when I'm forced to admit it," he said and grinned.

"Why wouldn't you want to?" At a loss for words, she gestured with her hands. "The name seemed *so* familiar, but I never connected it with you. I've seen the display, by the way. And now . . . this." She glanced from one piece to another. "Jace, your work is beautiful."

"It'll do."

"It'll more than do. It's absolutely exquisite. Oh, and the Browns! They must be in heaven, having you renovate The Glen."

"They're happy enough."

She caught a brief glimpse of pleasure in his eyes before his lashes came down. This was strange. He seemed too devilishly cocky to be the type to shrug off an acknowledgment of his talent. "You do this all here in your barn?"

"Yeah. Or I did. It kept me busy before I won the bed-and-breakfast contract."

"And now you don't have time for anything else, I'm sure."

"I squeeze in a few side jobs, here and there. Shelves and the like."

She smiled in his direction. "So, where do you live?"

He jerked his head. "Up there."

"The hayloft. Of course." Wasn't that where every reclusive artist hid out? But why was a man with his talent hiding behind a set of initials, in a barn, in an open pasture?

Secrets. More secrets. Warning bells went off like New Year's Eve fireworks.

Taking a deep breath, she glanced down and finally saw what he'd been trying to show her. Puppies. Six little balls of nothing but fluff lay in a slatted crate. Shredded newspaper and a gray-on-black flannel shirt provided a warm bed.

Chelsea reappeared, turned in three circles and settled against the back of the crate. The puppies rooted around their mother. Eden leaned forward and tentatively touched their soft fur.

"Oh, how precious." Her traitorous eyes misted. A crazy mood swing, of course. Nothing but hormones run rampant. Certainly not the worry that she had less maternal instincts than this dog.

She stood then, lifted her chin because it was the thing to do. Silently, Jace met her gaze, but she didn't want to explain the unexplainable, so she asked, "Do you want to show me the rack you had in mind?"

"Sure," he answered, his voice gruff, as if her female display of emotion had no place in his male dominion. He took a huge step back. "Be back in a second."

"Don't rush," Eden said. "I'm dying to try out the rocker."

"Be my guest." Jace wound his way around tool cabinets and shop caddies and scraps of lumber to the far corner of the barn. The same corner where a circular staircase led to the loft.

The thought of climbing those stairs quelled Eden's curiosity at seeing where he lived. Her aching feet were ready to call it a day, and the rocker couldn't have been more inviting.

The chair fit like Jace had molded the wood to her body. The seat reached the perfect height; the curve of the headrest sloped to perfection. She settled back and propped her feet on a small stool.

A T-shirt Jace must've tossed across the chair back earlier in the day fell on her shoulder. She brought the rocker to a stop and closed her eyes. The smell of rich sawdust came from the earth, as did the scent of clean male sweat clinging to the cotton.

She turned her head to the side and buried her nose in the folds of the cloth, feeling like an intruder, like an invader of Jace's privacy. But the simple comfort she derived from the act was a warmth she'd missed and hadn't realized to what extent.

This was the first time since Nate . . . since she shook off all remnants of that relationship and became her own person, that the need for companionship, friendship felt as vital as the need for physical sustenance.

The reaction shook her, and she laid the shirt aside. A big part of her move to Arbor Glen was a stand for independence. Not that she planned to live the rest of her life alone, but the timing was all wrong for what she was feeling, this emotional desire for a man. For Jace.

Hearing him approach, she opened her eyes. She couldn't have come up with anything more perfect if she'd commissioned the design. From a base resembling gnarled roots, the rack's straight shaft stood head high before branching out into four rods carved into vines.

It didn't look sturdy enough to support the wind, but she had no doubt it would work just fine, considering Jace stood leaning his full weight on it. Frowning, he rubbed one finger over a tiny scar on the wood, and Eden wondered if he had any idea that his soul shone in his eyes.

This was the real Jace Morgan. A craftsman, able to return a visage of life to dead wood. And she had no doubt he could do the same to a woman. Swallowing that thought, Eden got to her feet and reverently tested the feel of the wood. "Where did this come from?"

"I had a friend once. His wife had a thing for big floppy hats." He hesitated. What looked like regret clouded his eyes. "Terri and Kev moved away before I got around to finishing this."

"Are you sure you want to get rid of it?"

"Yeah. This wasn't what I was going to show you, but if you want it, it's yours. I didn't realize until I got back there that Chelsea's been using the base of the other rack to sharpen her teeth." At the mention of her name, Chelsea thumped her tail against the back of the crate.

"This is really perfect. How much do you want for it, and can we take it back tonight?"

He quoted her a price that staggered her for a second. Genius didn't usually come so cheap.

"I don't want to load it in the truck in the dark," Jace said. "I'll dig up a furniture pad and bring it over tomorrow."

"Sounds good. Between this and the shelving system, I should be set. Is that asking for a miracle?"

He shook his head. "I'll finish measuring for the shelves when I take you back tonight. I should be able to get everything done by the weekend after next."

"Great. This is so great," Eden exclaimed. "I'm going to have to thank Molly for sending you over." She walked a circle around the rack, marveling at the detailed scrollwork, then looked up and came to a complete stop.

Wedged in the corner of a worktable against the wall sat a tiny cradle. Her pulse racing, Eden crossed the floor to caress the curved rockers, the turreted headboard and the spindles carved into carousel animals.

"Jace," she whispered, the word hard to speak. She pressed her fingers to her lips and her other palm to the sudden ache at her breast. She turned her back to Jace, wanting nothing to ruin this moment for her. The piece could've been a merry-go-round, a child's first ride into imagination.

Jace had captured everything Eden felt about childhood in this one piece of miniature furniture, conveyed the whimsy, the fun, the laughter and the love with such exquisite perfection—all the things she'd vowed to provide for her children. All the things she'd had to turn her life upside down to make happen.

So why was she still so unsure that she'd done the right thing?

Balancing a checkbook was not the greatest way to start a day. Eden laid her glasses aside and, with the heels of her palms, rubbed the sleep from her eyes, no doubt making the circles beneath her lower lashes darker than they already were.

Though her hours now were strictly her own, her schedule was only marginally less demanding than the one she'd kept up in New York. The added anxiety of impending parenthood didn't help. She joked a lot about her physical condition, knowing she wasn't yet half as huge as she made out in her complaints.

The self-deprecating humor was a defense mechanism. She knew that, knew also that her self-confidence had taken a beating after being duped for three years by a married man. On top of her breakup with Nate, there was this huge lifestyle change she'd made to accommodate her status as a single mother of twins.

A girl could only take so much stress. She figured she was entitled to joke and to whine. Once or twice a day at least.

A sharp rap at the back door had her glancing around. A wisp of Chloe's blond hair shimmered in the seven A.M. sun. Eden glanced down at her cotton nightgown and shrugged. Looked like whine time was over. She padded to the back door, feeling like the brunt of a barefoot-and-pregnant joke.

"How was dinner?" she asked, holding open the door.

Chloe set the crate of dishes and a large straw carryall on the table. "Wonderful. Daddy ate every bit and wanted more."

Eden gave her a quick hug. "I'm so glad. Things with your dad will take time, Chloe."

"I know. We talked about it last night. About how much we both miss . . . her." She glanced away, her eyes glistening.

Eden wanted to soothe and turned to the old standby that seemed to work wonders. "Did you eat breakfast this morning?"

Chloe sniffed, and a childish smile crept across her mouth. "No. I was in such a hurry to get here, I forgot."

"What time do you have to be at school?"

She glanced at her black-banded wristwatch. "Not for an hour."

"Then sit down. I'll get the muffins out of the oven and we can talk."

"About the art project you need done?"

"That and *why* you were in such a hurry to get

here that you'd forget breakfast." Eden gathered up her paperwork and set it atop the pie safe for the time being. She made her way around the kitchen, pouring Chloe a glass of orange juice to start with.

Chloe pulled her sketchbook from her carryall. Eden sliced peaches and bananas, poached two eggs and listened to her guest's pencil scratch across the pad. She set the teakettle on the stove, then turned to study the teen, watching the fierce concentration with which Chloe worked.

Today she wore faded jeans and sandals, an oxford cloth shirt with sleeves cuffed to her elbows and a man's paisley print vest. Her hair was pulled back in a ponytail. A whisper of bangs brushed her brows. Beneath a frown of pure concentration, a light coat of mascara enhanced her eyes. With her lower lip caught between her teeth, her left-handed scrawl furiously attacked the page in front of her.

She looked like she was sixteen. She looked like an average teenage girl. She looked healthy and happy and exactly the way Eden wanted her daughter to look at that age. Smiling, Eden glanced up to catch Chloe's intense gaze on her face. Hmm.

Gathering the makings of breakfast, Eden set the table, ignoring the little voice telling her that Chloe was not a normal teen at all. She was a very wise old woman caught in a very young body, which was exactly what she wanted the town to think.

"Here we go," Eden said, pouring two tall glasses of milk. "The basic four food groups: protein, dairy, grains and fruit."

"You sound just like a mother," Chloe grumbled.

"Good. I'm supposed to. I figured I'd practice on someone I know, so you can tell me if I'm doing it right."

"Well, quit practicing. You've got it down perfect." Chloe folded the sketchbook and shoved it back in her bag.

"You're not going to let me see?"

"Not yet." Chloe reached for a muffin and centered it on her plate. "First, I want to know about the art project."

"I'm going to have my kitchen remodeled."

"You'll have to talk to your carpenter about that."

"I have talked to Jace. Now I want to talk to you."

"About what?" Chloe asked, eyeing the muffin from all sides.

"After the kitchen is painted, I'd like you to stencil the cabinets. Maybe do a border around the door facings and just below the ceiling."

Chloe scooped a spoonful of fruit from the bowl and glanced around the room. "A border would work. Leaves. Feathers. Maybe ribbons. And grapes."

"Grapes?"

"Grapes. But no flowers. Greens and blues, I think. Maybe a touch of rose."

"Sounds perfect." Eden sipped her tea, cradled the cup in her hands and, saving the best for last, plunged ahead. "But before you do that, I'd like you to paint a mural in the nursery."

Chloe's faced glowed, then mellowed, then darkened. She returned Eden's level gaze. "Is this because you feel sorry for me?"

"Why would I feel sorry for you?"

"I am an orphan."

"You're not an orphan. You have Nick." Eden squeezed Chloe's arm. "Chloe, I want you to do this because you have such a gift. You can bring my babies' room to life with color and magic and fun. I'll give you free rein to do what you want."

"Anything I want?"

Eden nodded, trusting Chloe with instincts that had never been stronger.

"Okay. This weekend I am free."

"Great." Eden stabbed her fork into her egg. "Now, tell me what has you in such a hurry this morning."

"I need your carpenter."

"What do you need with Jace?"

"Jenna has arranged for the advanced art class to have a display at the festival." Chloe spread peaches and bananas in a circle around the rim of her plate. She sliced her bran muffin into quarters and placed her egg in the center, making a four-point sun. She ate the peaches first.

"Back up a minute, Chloe. Who is Jenna?"

"My art instructor."

"Okay, so, what does the art show have to do with needing Jace?"

"Our projects must depict what Arbor Glen means to us."

"That's tough." Eden toyed with her muffin.

"No. It's simple." Chloe pressed her fists on either side of her plate. "Arbor Glen is the people I've been drawing for years. I have sketches of Obadiah making candles, my father sculpting a vase, Molly

baking brownies. I want to show the people altogether. As a whole. I need a special frame, one that
will unite the spirit of the town."

"So that's where Jace comes in."

"I know exactly what I want. But I don't know if
he'll do it. I cannot pay him with money." Chloe
pushed away from the table, then reached for her
milk and drained the glass. The bells between her
breasts tinkled as she moved, and Eden noticed then
that her shirt was entirely unbuttoned. It was held
in place by the vest and a lot of luck.

Such innocent sensuality made Chloe Chloe, and
Eden wondered how much trouble Nick had already
had from the boys. "What time can you be here
after school?"

Chloe wiped the milk from her upper lip. "Four."

"Okay. I close up at five. That'll give you an hour
to do your homework. Then we'll drive out to Jace's
place and see what we can work out." Eden took a
sip of her tea. When Chloe didn't respond, Eden
frowned, and after a long moment spent watching
the teen study her plate, Eden prompted, "Chloe?"

Chloe surged to her feet and paced the length of
the table, a strange energy humming in her path
before she dropped back into her chair. "What's it
like to feel another life growing in your body?"

Eden slowly placed her teacup in its saucer. "What
exactly is it you're asking?"

"I want to know everything. Does it hurt? Are you
scared? Do the babies move all the time? Can you
feel them?"

"It doesn't hurt and, no, I'm not scared. The babies sleep just like you and me, and when they're awake, yes, I can feel them. But just barely."

Chloe scooted her chair closer and dropped her voice to a pitch just above a whisper. "Did it feel good when you got pregnant? Did you like it?"

Eden hoped none of her alarm showed on her face. She wasn't ready for this aspect of motherhood. She hadn't conquered diapers and breastfeeding yet. She certainly wasn't ready for the birds and the bees.

"Are you asking about sex, Chloe?"

Chloe shook her head in clear frustration. "I know all about menstruation and ejaculation and eggs and sperm." She leaned closer, her hunger keen. "I want to know how it feels. I want to know about making love."

Eden swallowed hard. "Since you *want* to know, I guess that means you—"

"Yes, I'm still a virgin." A disgusted sigh fluttered her bangs.

"I'm glad to hear it." Eden paused for emphasis. "You wouldn't be planning on changing your status, would you?"

"With whom?"

"A boy at school, maybe?"

Chloe shuddered. "The boys at school are such boys. I want a man to teach me."

This conversation was growing worse by the minute. Eden groaned and pressed a forefinger and thumb to her temple. Then Benjamin made his presence known. And Eden saw the light. She took Chloe's hands and splayed them over her own taut belly.

Chloe's eyes widened. "It's so hard. I thought it would be soft. Like a pillow. Oh! Did you feel that?" She rubbed her palm down Eden's side. "There. I felt it again. Oh, Eden, this is wonderful. It's so . . . so . . . spiritual, I want to cry."

"Chloe, listen to me." She covered the girl's hands with her own. "I feel this constantly. And I'm only four months along. The babies don't want to sleep when I do. My back aches. Pains shoot down my legs. I have to go to the bathroom every thirty minutes. And right now I have it good.

"Once the babies are born I'll be lucky to sleep two or three hours a night. If I'm even luckier, they'll nap at the same time during the day. Maybe I'll catch up on my rest when they do. But more than likely I'll be working; I still have a business to run. A business that I need to keep a roof over my babies' heads."

Eden took a deep breath and went on. "Yes, sex is great. Making love is absolutely wonderful. But it means nothing if emotion is not involved, if some sort of responsibility or commitment does not exist."

She cupped Chloe's face in her palms. "Don't act on the heat of the moment. It's a fire that dies out quickly. And there's so much more to worry about than getting pregnant. Sex is a risk, Chloe. One you have to be old enough to take."

That said, Eden sat back.

Chloe leaned forward and kissed Eden's belly, then slung her carryall over her shoulder and headed for the back door. "I want to have a baby. But not now. Maybe one day, when I'm as grown up as you are."

Eden followed her to the door. "Then it might be a good idea to button your blouse before David Hansen or Eric Parsons or Lee Philips decides you're issuing an invitation."

She rolled her eyes in a decidedly teenage display of pique. "You're sounding like a mother again."

"Chloe . . ."

"I like to feel the wind on my skin." Leaping off the back porch, she turned a circle in the dew-covered grass. Eden caught a glimpse of one breast. "I like to feel free."

"Chloe . . ."

"I think I'll become a nudist."

Eden grimaced at Chloe's departing words, but noted with satisfaction that she buttoned at least four of the six buttons on her way out of the yard. Deciding this mothering business was going to be a royal test of her worth, Eden closed the back door and wondered if she should have a private talk with Nick Angelino.

Thirty minutes later, after cleaning the kitchen and relegating her paperwork to the desk drawer she'd labeled "TOMORROW," Eden gave up the battle with her hair and settled for a Chloe-style ponytail.

Morning light glowed golden in the east. Shrugging into her voluminous white terry robe, she stepped out to fetch her newspaper, only to have her breath catch tight in her chest.

He sat sprawled on her porch, leaning negligently against a support beam. One booted foot dragged the ground, a Styrofoam coffee cup balanced on his leg. The other boot rested flat on the porch, his wrist draped over his updrawn knee.

Steam curled in misty fingers from the creamy coffee. A matchstick dangled from the corner of his lower lip. He reached up to snatch it away, and his eyes met Eden's as he blew across the rim of the cup and sipped.

Eden blamed the fluttering around her legs on the capricious wind teasing her robe, the ripple in her stomach on the twins. Neither was true.

"Hi." Her voice was a breathless sigh.

In one supple motion, Jace gained his feet. "Hi, yourself."

"You should've knocked."

He rolled his shoulders in a loose shrug. "I figured you needed your rest. Besides"—he nodded his head toward the steaming coffee—"I haven't been here long."

"Mmm. That smells good," she said on a wistful note, inhaling a breath of coffee-fragrant air. "I can't remember the last time I drank the real stuff."

"You want half of this?" Jace offered.

She shook her head. "Herbal tea for me. Other than that, I stick to juice and milk. As soon as I get rid of this, however"—she patted her stomach—"I plan on drinking a gallon or two."

Jace's heart-flopping smile, no less potent even at such an early hour, reached all the way to his dark-fringed eyes, the corners crinkling in deep lines of amusement. "Then I'd be privileged to buy you the first cup."

"It's a date," Eden said, before weighing the implied familiarity of such a statement. Since she couldn't take back words already spoken she shrugged it off, hoping Jace would do the same. No sense complicating matters further. "Have you eaten breakfast?"

"I grabbed a kolache down at Molly's a while ago. I figured I'd get an early start before you opened up." He yawned, an incredibly sexy early morning sound that lent rise to the question of how he'd spent his after-dark hours. He thumped his matchstick into the street and swallowed a mouthful of coffee.

Eden walked out another step. "Let me grab the newspaper and we can go in."

"I'll get it," Jace offered.

"Thank you," she said softly and, taking the paper from him, turned toward the door. A second later she heard the tread of his heavy bootsteps. Something akin to delight rippled all the way to her bare toes. Ridiculous, she told herself, even as a smile played across her lips.

Dropping the paper on the kitchen table, she tightened her belt as best she could around her nonexistent waist. Determined to ignore her elemental reaction to Jace—a response totally inappropriate for a woman in her condition—she headed for the stairs, only to find him taking up most of the narrow hallway.

He retreated a step and pressed his back against the wall. Eden tried to slide by, but the house was old, the hallway close and her belly no match for the combination.

"A gallon of grease won't help this tight squeeze, Morgan. You're just gonna have to put it in reverse."

The hallway was dark enough that she didn't have to see his face. That meant he couldn't see hers, either. Just as well. He'd smelled too much like early morning man and she knew her appreciation burned red on her face. It seemed like forever before he reached her doorway.

She ducked her head and scooted on by. "Make yourself at home. I'll be down in a few minutes."

By the time she'd found what she'd once thought to be unshakable composure, Jace was busy in the shop. Eden headed for her workroom. Above the whir of her machine she could hear the whine of a power saw and spurts of hammering coming from his direction.

When ten o'clock rolled around, she'd completed all but the finishing touches of appliqué on two more jumpers like the one she'd designed for Molly. She shut off the serger, gathered up her handiwork, dropped it along with her sewing basket on the counter and crossed the room to turn the sign on the door to OPEN.

She met Jace coming back in, a small shop-vac in hand. "I'm impressed. The man vacuums, too."

Jace dispensed a playful scowl in return. Eden watched him run the vacuum across the sawdusted corner of the floor.

The motor's roar at last wound down and Jace snapped the vacuum cord. After lugging the vac back to his truck, he gathered up the drop cloths. Next he fetched his tools.

All the while Eden watched him come and go until

she realized he had nothing to come back for. She spun around and headed out the door.

He was just climbing into the driver's seat when she reached the truck. She pulled open the passenger-side door and, not bothering to hide her consternation, asked, "Are you leaving?"

"Yeah. It'll be easier to work during the hours you're closed. I don't like people stepping over and around me, and I need to run out to The Glen." He turned the key and gunned the motor, flipping through his pocket-size notebook. "I'll be back this evening."

She knew her relief was as plain as the proverbial nose on her face when he said, "Don't worry. I'll have the shelves done in time for the festival." He slapped his notebook shut and clipped it to the visor overhead. The motion pulled his army green T-shirt tight across his shoulders.

Eden pulled her gaze away from his body. "Chili tonight?"

He stared straight ahead. A quirky grin crept across his mouth as he shook his head and chuckled. "Creole. And now chili. You a victim of those strange pregnant cravings?"

It wasn't until he'd agreed to dinner and driven away, rooster tails of smoky white gravel spraying out from beneath his tires, that Eden realized Jace's laughing comment was the first reference he'd made to her condition.

And that she'd forgotten to mention that she'd be seeing him as soon as Chloe got out of school.

FOUR

Jace shoved the pencil behind his ear, grabbed the T-shirt he'd discarded earlier and, with two quick swipes, dried his chest. Sweat dripped from the ends of his hair and ran down his back. The bandanna tied around his forehead was soaked.

He exchanged it for a dry one and slung the shirt around his shoulders. Reaching for a scrub plane, he braced one palm on a sheet of white pine and breathed deep, inhaling the smell of green wood and sun.

He loved working outdoors. It still amazed him that, after ten years cooped up in a Dallas high-rise, he'd managed to escape with his sanity intact. Busting his butt may have earned him professional recognition, acceptance from his colleagues and a lot of bets paid off in beer, but it had never brought him the inner peace he found when working with wood.

After six years of school and five years of corporate employment, he'd made a conscious move to reclaim his life. For the last thirty-six months, he'd had no one to answer to but himself, no one breathing down his neck, no one to compete with.

The competition drought had given him the most trouble at first, but he'd gotten used to being his own measure of success. Now he wouldn't live any other way.

He had his barn and his dog—not to mention freedom and five acres. A man could do a lot worse, but he couldn't do much better. Unless he were to make peace and apologize to the three best friends he'd pretty much tossed from his life like yesterday's front page.

Yeah, he had more than a little unfinished business he needed to get to soon.

Sawdust tickling his nose and a new rush of old guilt giving him an elbow jab in the side, Jace made one final pass with the plane. The sound of a car engine intruding on his silence brought his head up.

Squinting, he glanced up to see a black Volvo bouncing down his drive. He tossed the plane into his toolbox, dusted his hands on his jeans and waited.

The face that finally came into view behind the tinted windows of the boxy black machine belonged to the center of his unwanted thoughts of late. He tensed, relaxed, tensed again. Made a mental check of the source.

Yep. Eden. City-girl Eden. And to think that for the next couple of weeks he'd be stuck working inside. With her. In that old house that seemed smaller every time he measured its walls.

She pulled to a stop next to his work truck and killed the engine. Her door swung open, her feet hit the dirt and she stepped from the car. More colors of red than he knew existed glinted in her hair. Sunlight only served to highlight individual strands. He saw cherry, sandalwood, cedar and more. He wondered if Nick Angelino had ever done a portrait of Eden. Wondered if the artist would do it as a favor.

Wondered why he was being so stupid.

Two car doors slammed in quick succession and he finally realized that Eden wasn't alone. Chloe was with her. He started to put on his shirt, then decided against it and raised his chin. They'd invaded his manly domain. They'd have to deal with the savage beast.

Eden picked her way over the uneven turf, glancing from the rocky ground to his half-clothed body. He resisted sucking in his gut when he realized where her gaze lingered.

Some savage. Some beast.

"Ladies." He nodded, grinned. "If I'd known you were coming, I'd've dressed for the occasion." He hooked his thumbs in his belt loops. "You two sightseeing?"

"What a fabulous place, Jace." Eden shaded mischievous eyes with one hand. "Now that I can see what I missed last night, I'm glad I came back. The view today is"—she paused, then added—"definitely worth the trip."

Great. Just what he needed. Flirtation from a woman who already had him tied in knots.

Chloe signaled Eden closer with a crook of one finger. "Eden, you know that lesson I wanted this morning?"

Eden clapped one hand over Chloe's mouth and glared at the girl. "Don't even think about it."

"Are you sure?" Chloe cast an interested glance at Jace—a glance that had him wishing he'd put on his shirt.

"Yes. I'm sure," Eden said. "Now, where are your papers?"

"Oh. I'll get them." With only one backwards peek between the fingers hiding her eyes, Chloe jogged to the car and rummaged through the large straw bag she pulled from the backseat.

Returning his attention to Eden, Jace crossed his arms, balanced on his wide-spread feet and waited—though, knowing the two females he was dealing with here, he wasn't sure waiting would bring satisfaction. "You gonna let me in on the joke?"

"No joke. A favor. Chloe needs a favor, Jace." Eden shot a quick glance toward the car, then lowered her voice. "But I'll be glad to pay you."

He gave Eden his full attention. Not because of the money, but because even a savage could sense the import of Chloe's request. "What kind of favor?"

"I wouldn't bother you if it wasn't so important to her." She smoothed her blouse down over her growing belly. The swell was barely noticeable, and he wouldn't have noticed it at all if she hadn't drawn his attention with her hands.

He wondered if she was comforting her baby, soothing herself or somehow empathetically protecting Chloe.

And he found his carefree mood fading, but only because he'd moved closer and could smell nothing now but apricots and Eden. *Inside. With her. In that old house.* "What's the favor?"

"Here," Chloe called, waving a handful of papers at Jace on her return jog from the car.

He took them from her, ten sheets, various sizes, all blank. He turned them over again to be sure. Yep. Blank. Looking up, he asked, "What's this?"

"These are the sizes of the drawings I need framed."

This was about frames? For drawings? That was easy enough. "Why don't you check The Emporium? I'm sure John has frames to fit."

"No." She shook her head, as if agitated. "I need one frame."

Jace frowned, working to understand what she wanted. "Like a shadowbox?"

"One frame. Separate pictures. Each extending from the next." She traced an elongated shape in the air with her hands.

Jace gave up, handing her back the sheets. "Show me what you mean."

With an exasperated sigh, Chloe plucked the pencil from behind his ear, grabbed the papers from his hand, slapped the stack down on the sheet of pine and proceeded to draw. What she sketched was a series of connecting squares and rectangles overlapping one another from corner to corner.

Jace scratched his stubbled jaw, then plowed his fingers through his damp hair. He pointed to the papers. "And these are the sizes of your pictures?"

"Exactly. I measured each one."

"Okay." He blew out a long breath. "Let's lay them out and see what we get."

The finished product was five feet long and two feet tall. Jace whistled long and low.

"Is there a problem?" Eden asked.

"Depends on where you plan to hang this thing." He glanced at Chloe for an answer.

The teen looked more than a little put out. "Jenna will display our work on the back wall of The Emporium during the Spring Fest."

"Who's Jenna?" Jace asked, feeling like every question he asked spawned another. Then Eden laid her hand on his arm and the anxiety he'd caught from Chloe became a knot of unholy nerves in his stomach.

"Jenna is Chloe's art teacher," Eden explained, squeezing his forearm lightly once before moving her fingers away.

"Got it." *Inside. That old house. With her.* He turned to Chloe. "Is she setting up a Peg-board? Plywood? An easel?"

"I don't know," she replied, offering a typical teenager shrug.

Nothing like the facts to make a job easy. Oh, well. This wasn't rocket science. "Since you don't know, we'd better make it as lightweight as possible."

"That means you can do it?"

"Sure."

Chewing on one ragged thumbnail, Chloe focused on the layout. "How many days will it take?"

"Depends on how fast Eden wants her shelves." When he saw the quick flash of concern in Eden's eyes, he added, "But I can probably do it in a couple of evenings."

"Perfect." Chloe threw her arms around Eden in a big hug. "Thanks, Eden."

"I'm not the one you should thank," Eden responded, winking at Jace over Chloe's shoulder.

Jace shifted on his feet and acknowledged the sudden urge to step back just as Chloe launched herself his way. Breath whooshed from his lungs. A sharp grunt followed as Chloe's knee connected with his thigh seconds before his butt hit the ground.

Straddling his lap, she wrapped both arms around his neck and squeezed. His elbows bolstered both their weights, which was good. He wasn't sure of the best place to put his hands. Or the best way to move without dumping his passenger to the ground.

His security system solved the problem for him. At the dog's sudden, territorial bark, Chloe scrambled to her feet. She turned toward the barn, pressing her hands to her heart as if in awe. "Look. It's a silver wolf."

Jace stood, dusted the seat of his pants. *A silver wolf?* A quick glance at Eden and he knew she wasn't going to be any help, standing there barely stifling a giggle. He glared at her with the straightest face he could manage while speaking to Chloe. "Chelsea's a malamute."

The teen totally ignored Jace's correction, reaching widespread slender fingers toward the dog. "I hear her speaking to me. I see it in her eyes." She turned an imploring gaze to Jace. "Can I pet her?"

"Approach her slowly. Let her smell your hand so she'll know you're of the friendly variety."

"Whatever," Chloe said, with the forced indulgence of sixteen. She tiptoed toward the barn.

Jace turned to Eden. "That is one weird chick."

Eden's expression was a portrait in indulgence. "She's sixteen, Jace. She's female. And on top of that, she's incredibly creative."

"Sounds like a serious right-brained mixture to me."

"Would that be experience talking?"

Jace spread his arms wide. "Creative I'll buy. But you see anything female here, you let me know."

Her glance took in the length of his body, the expanse of his homestead, his expression. She arched an inquisitive brow. "Actually, I see a decided lack of anything female around here."

"And that's a problem?"

"Not for me." She added crossed arms to her question. "Is it for you?"

Jace let the query hang because he wasn't sure he wanted to get into this with a woman he wanted to get into this with. She was pregnant, she belonged to someone—or had some time recently. She was a city girl; she missed the life and might be going back. And he found himself thinking about her anyway.

If anything was a problem for him, it was Eden Karr.

"Between you and Chloe and Chelsea, I'd say I'm currently overdosed on female."

Eden didn't counter, but instead took a longer

look around. "Molly said you spend most of your time out here by yourself."

Jace sighed. "I guess you think that's a problem, too."

"Nope. What I think is that business must keep you busy."

"You can say that again," Jace answered honestly before heading for the storage building behind his barn to see what he could do about helping Chloe.

Eden followed, her footsteps crunching the trail of sticks Chelsea had dropped on the overgrown path. Swinging open the door to the shed, he stepped inside the gloomy darkness.

Musty and damp, the air hung over the room. Jace moved first one box and then another, away from the two-by-two window. The floor creaked as Eden stepped inside.

Her shadow fell over him from her place in the doorway. "I know who you are, Jace."

He stiffened and rolled aside a keg of nails. "I told you who I was. You recognized my work at The Old Pine Box."

"No. That's not what I meant." Her shadow moved as she took another step into the room. "Six years ago I was assigned to cover a fashion show in Dallas. It was canceled, so I accompanied a friend to the dedication of the Farriday Building."

Jace shoved his hands into his jeans pockets, stared out the grimy square of glass and shifted his weight between feet. Looked like his gig was up.

"Dallas had never seen anything like it," Eden went on. "The papers called the architect a perfec-

tionist, able to stop back and observe the small piece
in the big visual scene, able to let form follow func-
tion. But that architect, one J.B. Morgan, was absent
from his own unveiling. Another member of the
firm cut the ribbon."

Yep. He'd been too busy working on his next project to celebrate his Farriday success. "He couldn't
make it. Something came up."

As if she hadn't heard him—which he knew she
had by the roll of her eyes—Eden continued.
"When we got back to New York, my friend dug up
everything she could find on J.B. Morgan.

"It seems the Farriday Building was the first project this Morgan had designed. He was headed for
architectural stardom." Palms up, she turned a circle where she stood, then met his gaze. "And now
here he is, hiding out in a barn in the middle of a
pasture."

Jace jerked a carpenter's apron from the top of
one crate. He wasn't sure how much he wanted to
tell Eden about the reasons he'd left Dallas. It wasn't
like he was particularly proud of the way he'd
stepped on everyone he knew while climbing that
ladder of success.

"Wait. Let me guess," he settled on saying. "You
have a problem with that, too."

"No. I don't," she said, her voice soft behind him.
"But you do."

Her words landed hard. He turned then and all
he saw was her silhouette backlit by the sun stream-
ing in through the door. She had the shape of an
ordinary woman. A plain average woman, which was

a joke in itself. There was nothing plain or average about Eden.

The tiny, cluttered room grew smaller. And instead of dust motes dancing in the shafts of light, the sparks in her hair caught his eye. Instead of creaks and groans as the old building shifted and settled, her unsteady intake of breath rustled in the still air. Instead of wood, he smelled woman, a mixture soft and sweet and scented with friendship and home.

"The Farriday Building is exquisite," she said quietly. "You must be so proud."

Jace stood still, not certain what to say. Sure, pride was a part of what he felt. But there were so many other emotions connected to those years that pride seemed to have taken a backseat. He'd let down Robert and Kevin and Marv. And he'd let down himself by failing his friends.

A building didn't seem like such a be-all-and-end-all in the larger scheme of life. Sure his name went up on the dedication plaque, but he'd only been part of a larger team. He knew that now, but he sure hadn't taken time to appreciate his assistants and co-workers then. Put simply, he'd been a first-class ass.

In desperate need of breathing room, Jace headed for the storage shed's door. Eden refused to move out of his way. Fine. Two could play this stubborn game.

He slung the apron over his shoulder, stopped when he reached her and propped his fist on the doorframe above her head. He did nothing but breathe for the next minute, making sure she was as aware as he of his gut pressed tight to her gently rounded belly.

Her cheeks flushed and her eyes burned bright, and Jace resolutely refused to look away. "I don't think I'll have time for chili tonight. If I'm gonna do this frame for Chloe, I'd better scrounge up what I need this evening."

"Fine," she whispered and pushed back against the shed.

Leaning forward, he lifted a strand of her hair and worried it between his fingers. "I can't give up what I have here, Eden. You may miss the bright lights and big city, but I don't care to see either again. Don't think by reminding me of the successes I've had that you can change who I am. Or the way I've chosen to live my life."

Her throat convulsed as she swallowed. "I'm not asking you to change anything."

"Are you sure?" Jace counted the freckles on her nose, the sprinkling across her cheekbones, the random dusting across her neck. When he found his gaze traveling lower, his mind wandering lower still, he dropped her hair and stepped into the sun.

Before he stepped into her arms.

Jace didn't come for chili that night, and though he arrived in a standoffish mood at daybreak, he didn't refuse Eden's offer of scrambled eggs and biscuits. Two nights later he stayed for a hurried meal of stuffed baked potatoes and picked up a dozen kolaches from Molly's the morning after.

The routine continued through the weekend. But Jace never looked at her again the way he'd looked at her in the doorway of his shed. After spending the past six days with the man, Eden felt they were more in tune than many married couples.

Still, nothing she'd learned went deeper than the surface. Since that one brief confrontation, Jace had deflected her every effort to pry. What she knew was to pass the cream for his coffee; he, never to butter her toast.

She knew more, as well. That he'd want a quart of iced tea by three, then nothing but beer with supper. And since lunch wasn't her best time of day, he managed to have an extra sandwich in his lunchbox, even when he didn't eat.

When she slipped her shoes off her swollen feet one afternoon, he teased her about her size-eight Jumbo the Elephants. And her woman's intuition told her he wore an extra large—in everything.

Monday morning she woke late with a headache, a backache and a heartache that defied explanation. Broody and bloated from head to toe, she wanted to stay in bed and wallow in her misery. Even better, to soak in a tub of apricot-scented bubbles, eat a pan of butter brownies and reread her favorite romance novel.

Unfit company for man, beast or even herself, she slipped into a huge shapeless T-shirt dress and padded barefoot to the kitchen for a muffin and tea. Why had she thought relocating and changing careers had been a smart move?

And why in the world did she think she'd be a

good mother? She couldn't even take care of herself.
How was she supposed to take care of a business
and a family when she couldn't get beyond the need
for a good cry?

It was an eat-a-worm day all around.

So, when Jace knocked on her kitchen door at
ten, she purposefully kept her outward reaction to
one of surprise, even though deep inside she welcomed him home. The screen door creaked as she
pulled it open. "I hate you, you know."

Two steps brought him up her stairs and into her
kitchen. Three more took him the width of the
room. Arms crossed over his chest, he leaned back
against the refrigerator and gave her that sexy Jace
Morgan grin. "Good morning to you, too."

Prying her gaze from the suede tunic sheathing
his wide shoulders, Eden swallowed hard and
pushed the door shut behind her. "What I mean is,
do you never take a day off? No one who puts in
the hours you do has a right to look so . . ." *Gorgeous,* her brain supplied, ". . . rested," she forced
herself to say.

Jace shrugged, stretching the fabric even tighter.
"I don't take many days off. Not scheduled, anyway."

"What do you mean?" She stacked her hands on
the door behind her and leaned back, her protruding stomach protruding even more.

Jace's gaze slid away. He ran one finger over the
porcelain knob of the cabinet door beside him. "I
work at my own pace. I don't punch a clock. When
I'm tired, I stop. It's that simple."

"So, what are you doing here today? You're certainly not dressed for work."

"I have a delivery to make in Farmersville." He shifted his weight from one foot to the other. "But I was hoping we could do some business first."

Eden pushed off from the door, determined to finish her breakfast dishes, equally determined to ignore the way Jace Morgan filled her kitchen. And the way she felt less blue when he was around. "I don't know, Morgan. I can't afford to do much more business with you."

"It'll only cost you time."

She turned, soapsuds clinging to her hands. "Time?"

"Yep. It's called bartering."

"What could I possibly have to barter with that would interest you?" she asked, then wished she hadn't. His heated look flared between them, wordlessly answering her question. Finally, he turned. The back seam of his shirt gaped open, revealing taut muscles and smooth skin.

Too much skin, to Eden's way of thinking. With unsteady hands, she rinsed her teacup and pulled the stopper from the drain. "Bartering, huh? Like, in exchange for my services as a seamstress, you'll knock a couple bucks off your estimate to redo my kitchen?"

Lifting the cheesecloth covering the basket on her stove, Jace helped himself to a cinnamon roll. "If that's what you want."

What she wanted right now was best not put into words. She watched the final swirl of bubbles vanish down the drain, wiped down the lip of the sink and dried her hands. "No. What I want is to ride into Farmersville with you. I've got an order to pick up at Calico Corners."

He looked up, half the roll in his mouth. "That's it?"

"C'mon, Jace. Ten minutes of my time isn't worth much more than a ride." She tossed the towel on the countertop.

"Sounds like a helluva deal to me."

"Then let's take a look at the damage."

Jace licked cinnamon glaze from his fingers, braced his palms on a chair back and bent at an angle that gave Eden a clear, close view of his back. Her fingers trembled for no good reason. At least none she allowed herself to consider.

Skimming the buckskin with a light touch, she tested the strength of the seam's worn edges. Heat from Jace's skin breathed over her hands, a seductive invitation to slip her fingers inside the shirt.

She closed her eyes. The scent of leather and man seeped into her loneliness. Then Benjamin kicked, reminding her not to be stupid again, and she backed a step away. "Fabric looks tough enough. I think the thread just gave up the ghost."

Jace glanced back. "So, can you fix it?"

"Sure."

"Now?"

"Now?" she repeated.

He nodded. "The bed of my truck's loaded. I need to get over to Farmersville before it rains."

The sunlight shining through her kitchen window dimmed on cue.

"I don't think I have time to drive home and change." When she only stared, he went on to say, "I can go like this if you don't have time."

Eden shook off her trance. How bad could it actually be to have Jace undress in her house? She'd seen him shirtless just last week. Then they'd been outdoors, with acres of breathing room. Now they were in her house. Alone. With gloomy skies increasing the intimacy.

"I have time," she assured him, then held out her hand and held her breath. He slipped out of the shirt and, before she allowed herself more than the briefest glimpse of a male belly dusted with black hair, she headed for her workroom.

His moccasins whispered over the hardwood floor behind her, the sound a gentle coaxing of her senses, a sweet song to her ears. She felt his presence like a wildness inside her. His shirt grew warm in her hands.

Shoving back the curtained partition, she tossed the shirt onto her sewing table, gestured for Jace to sit in the rattan side chair and headed for the cherry cupboard in the corner.

The top drawer held hundreds of spools of thread and, in her state of klutziness and nerves and hormonal melancholy, she nearly toppled the contents to the floor.

Especially when she sensed Jace move to the window behind her. Eyes closed, she took a small backwards step in his direction, close enough to indulge herself in the warmth of his bare skin, the scent of naked man and the subtle need to be near another human being.

It was crazy, this weakness shifting through her. Crazy. Insane. A gut awareness she hadn't counted on. She'd never expected to come up against a man who'd make her want this way again.

Be honest, Eden. A man who makes you want in a way you've never wanted before.

"How far away is the rain?" she asked, hating the way her voice shook.

"Storm's coming from the west. It won't hit for another hour."

His voice wrapped around her, safety and security rolled up into one. The intensity of her desire deepened. Oh, God, she didn't need this. Taking a deep breath, she slammed the thread drawer in punctuation.

"Great. Give me ten minutes and you're on your way." Ten minutes was no time. Her mood would probably swing again in the next five. She grabbed her glasses from her sewing basket and settled into the chair.

"There's hot tea and more cinnamon rolls in the kitchen if you'd like to wait in there," she offered, hoping he'd accept.

"No, thanks." The windowseat cushion rustled beneath his weight. "I like this room."

Rust-colored thread aimed through the eye of the needle, Eden adjusted the machine's tension and reached for her pincushion. "It's my favorite room in the house." She aligned the edges of the shirt seam. "Well, besides the bathroom. The clawfoot tub upstairs is big enough to swim in."

"There was a room with a windowseat like this in the house I grew up in. It was supposed to be a formal sort of living area, but nothing about my family was formal.

"My sister and I had a lot of friends, and the room ended up being a hangout." Eden heard the latch click then heard Jace push up the window. The old wood frame creaked and groaned in protest.

"Problem was, my mother tossed so many pillows onto the windowseat that no one could sit there. We ended up sprawled everywhere else, though. Sofa, chairs, floor, coffee table," he said with a laugh.

"Sounds like my kind of room. And my kind of family," Eden ventured, wondering more than she should have—and for no logical reason—about what Jace had been like as a child. If he saw his family often.

And why he'd traded a life teeming with friends for the one he lived alone. "Do you miss that? Having friends around all the time?"

Silence filled the room. Leaves whispered and swished against the window screen. Tires rolled over the joints in the road, a synchronized click to the tick of a clock. The windowseat groaned beneath Jace's shifting weight. And Eden waited.

"Yeah. I do," he finally said, but he said no more, and his tone left no room for questions.

As curious as she was, Eden knew when to leave well enough alone. She'd pry again another time. Flipping off the machine, she stashed her glasses back in her sewing basket. "Let's see if this is going to hold," she said, then made the mistake of looking his way.

Jace lounged like a man who made a living at it. His moccasin-clad feet, crossed at the ankles, extended a foot off the seat. His legs filled his jeans with symmetrical perfection. A braided belt of leather and turquoise circled his waist.

The thumbs he'd hooked through his belt loops tugged at his waistband, drawing her gaze to the whorl of hair growing low on his belly. And to his zipper, and the pure male magic outlined beneath.

She caught her breath.

He turned his head. His glance snagged hers and pulled.

A gust of breeze kicked the clouds across the sky and sunlight bathed the room. Jace rolled to his feet, and Eden's gaze searched out what she couldn't get enough of. Corded muscle and skin kissed copper by the sun. The breadth of his chest amazed her, especially as his belly below was sleek and spare. His build was that of a hard-working man.

Soft spring breezes brought wisteria, jasmine and honeysuckle inside. Jace's hair ruffled at his neck. His scent reached her, too. She drowned in the smells and accepted the truth. The man in Jace beckoned the woman in her.

"Here." She handed him the shirt.

"Thanks." He took it from her and pulled it on.

She clenched her hands. The need to touch him sizzled in the tips of her fingers, screamed in the hollow of her heart. His hair caught in the neckline of the tunic. Desire won out over reason. She reached up to free the strands.

Black satin slid over her fingers. The stubble on his jaw grazed her wrist. She touched his cheek, ignoring the sirens in her mind. Wrong or right, this connection mattered more than her next breath.

Jace's eyes grew sleepy, seductive. He mirrored her action, his palm rough against her cheek. So easy. So natural. So simple to move the one short step into his arms.

Thunder rumbled low. The sky darkened, breaking the spell. As much as she longed to do otherwise, she moved back. "Sounds like your hour's been cut short."

Jace seemed indecisive, hesitant even, like what had just passed between them had confused him as much as it had her. Like he couldn't put a name to the thick tension in the room without calling it what neither of them wanted: involvement, attraction, the beginning of attachment.

Lightning flashed. Jace blinked, stepped back. "We'd better get going. Water-damaged furniture isn't likely to bring the price I have hanging on those pieces."

If they were going now, she needed to get dressed. She headed for the stairs. "What pieces are you delivering today?"

"I've got a Shaker table and six chairs. Plus the cradle."

Eden stopped on the first step. The cradle? He was selling the cradle? Of course he was selling the cradle. This was business, after all. Still, she didn't think she could bear to see that particular piece sold. Why, she couldn't say. But since when did hormones think with logic?

Turning, she pressed her fists against the small of her back. "On second thought, Jace, I don't think I'm up to the trip. Maybe you could stop by and pick up my order?"

He frowned. "Are you sure?"

"Yeah. Let me get the list." They walked into the shop. Eden grabbed the slip of paper and handed it to Jace. "Marian can double check the items, but she should have them ready. You don't have to stop by on your way back. Just bring them over tomorrow." She pulled open the front door but didn't step out.

"If you're sure . . ."

She nodded.

"Okay. Thanks." Jace jogged to his truck, climbed into the cab and was off with a wave.

Eden gripped the door. She watched the Ford as it turned from Main onto Highway 37. Then she went back inside to spend the rest of her day feeling sorry for herself.

It was definitely an eat-a-worm day.

FIVE

Thursday afternoon Eden jerked awake so abruptly that the brass headboard jarred the wall behind it.

After rubbing the sleep from her eyes, she closed the portfolio spread across her lap, then searched for her glasses, finding them wedged between two pillows beneath her sketch pad.

Benjamin woke seconds later and prodded his sister into action. Bethany complied with enthusiasm, planting a tiny foot into Eden's side.

Surprised to find her entire family on the same schedule, she scooted off the bed and into her shoes, yawned and stretched.

She should've thought to set her alarm, though she'd yet to need one since her afternoon *naps* weren't as much about sleep as about appeasing Molly.

And Molly always called from the bottom of the stairs once she heard Eden moving around.

Of course, Molly had no way of knowing that Eden timed her *naps,* spending the hour a day propped up in bed, her notebook computer and spreadsheets and fashion catalogs across her lap.

Today was a costly exception.

Though she felt rested enough to make it through this evening's monthly town meeting, making up the lost worktime later tonight would definitely foul up tomorrow.

After a quick stop in the bathroom to repair her mussed hair, she headed for the stairs, noting the lateness of the hour from the angle of sunlight slanted across the hallway.

It was way past closing time. She'd obviously been pushing herself harder than pregnancy allowed if she could so easily sleep the afternoon away.

Stepping off the bottom stair, she walked into the shop. Instead of Molly at her post, Eden found Jace sitting on the stool behind the register.

No, not sitting. Sleeping—his chin balanced in his palm, his elbow parked on the counter, his head braced sideways against the wall.

She first wished for a camera, then suppressed a grudging envy for his ability to sleep through anything. Her third thought brought a frown.

With Jace sleeping through anything, and Molly nowhere in sight, who was minding the store?

Tiptoeing her way to the front door, Eden noticed the sign in the window turned to CLOSED. For a brief second she wondered what time Molly had left and if the sign had turned away any business. Oh well. Spilled milk and all . . .

The thought of milk had her stomach grumbling, and now she was in for a late supper. She needed to get moving or she'd miss the town meeting.

Before she could leave, however, she had to wake her carpenter.

Her carpenter. Eden smiled at Chloe's epithet, which had stuck. Ink-black lashes cast shadows on his cheeks. A sprinkling of sawdust powdered his hair and sifted over his T-shirt like glitter on velvet.

He looked . . . endearing, little-boy cute and like he hadn't a care in the world. She wanted to wrap him in a soft woven throw, tuck him securely in a comfy feather bed and curl up at his side.

A swift kick from Benjamin snapped her from dangerous fantasy back to the present. Anyone who could sleep through anything, not to mention make her ache to snuggle when she had a life and a business to get on track, deserved to be awakened with a dirge of music.

She pulled the front door open on a prayer. Nothing. She eased it inward another two inches. Nothing. Her gaze still on Jace, she scooted the door back a good foot and a half. That should do the trick.

Instead of the clatter and clank she'd grown to dread, however, the sweet strains of a lullaby floated on the air, the simple notes few and delicate, but oh so sweet. Suddenly and disgustingly misty-eyed, she closed her eyes and listened.

"I found that in one of the shops in Farmersville. Thought you might like it better." Jace's voice, husky with sleep, drifted across the room.

He scooted away from the counter, the stool legs scraping tracks across the floor, his boots thudding hard in that determined step she'd grown accustomed to hearing when he worked in her house.

Eden blinked and closed the door. She wanted to ask so many things—why he'd been thinking of her? what did he think of her? did he think of her often?—but none of those questions came.

It seemed the more time she spent around Jace, the more often she tripped over her tongue. She was a strong and independent businesswoman and he reduced her to a blubbering fool.

Taking a shaky breath, she leaned her forehead against the sturdy support of the wooden door. It was a good thing she was having her children all at one time. She didn't think she could go through the emotional upheaval of pregnancy again. Content one minute. Teary the next. And of course that's where these rubber-band emotions came from. Her mood swings were all about pregnancy and not about Jace at all.

She took a deep breath. "The chime is wonderful. And I love it."

"Good. I'm glad."

His voice came low and deep from behind her. She suppressed a shiver of . . . what? Fear? Attraction? Desire? No. It was hormones. Nothing more. She turned, determined once and for all to climb out of this emotional pit.

"Buying gifts is not part of our contract, you know. Neither are the errands you run for me. Or the lunches you bring me. Or the way you helped Chloe with her art project." She arched a brow. "Okay, Jace. What're you after?"

He crossed both arms and fought a grin. "You think I'm after something?"

She moved a step away and gave him a sidelong glance. "Maybe. I think so. Are you?"

This time he laughed. "Just working to put another line on my résumé."

"Right." She rolled her eyes, pulled aside the lace curtain on the windowed front door and looked out. "Like J. B. Morgan needs another line on his résumé."

"I don't use J.B.'s résumé."

His tone was so serious that she let the curtain fall and gave him her full attention instead. "Why not?"

Jace glanced away, down at the floor, and shoved his hands in his pockets. "Let's just say I'm not too fond of J. B.'s business practices."

Interesting, Eden thought, and narrowed a teasing eye. "Is this a Jekyll-and-Hyde thing?"

A trace of humor flickered through his eyes. He stepped closer, bringing with him the scent of dark nights, campfires and stars. The fit of his body she remembered from the day in his shed. The quick glance he gave her burned to her toes, and she knew he remembered, too. She held her breath as he leaned nearer to peer out the window at her side.

"Depends on what you're feeding me tonight," he said and smiled.

Eden glared. "I may have to hurt you for that."

"Promise?"

His profile was so temptingly close and her fingertips ached to touch him. Eden stepped away. "You know, Jace, I think it would be a good idea if we kept this business."

Jace glanced at the sawdust on his shirt, inclined his head toward the tools on the floor, looked back at Eden. "This isn't business?"

Moving to sit on the sill of the bay window, Eden sighed. "You're right. It is. And until I get The Fig Leaf established, business is all I have time for."

"No time to stop and smell the roses?"

She shook her head. "I have a great olfactory memory, though. That'll have to do me for a while. For now it's full steam ahead."

"And you don't think the rest of your life suffers? When you push yourself like that?"

It hadn't before. But everything about her life now was so new that she gave him the only answer she could. "I don't let it suffer."

"That's a hell of a tall order," Jace finally replied.

"I think of it more as an affirmation." She laughed quietly. "Maybe when I've been my own boss as long as you have, I'll say it and mean it."

Jace sent a lingering glance out the window over Eden's head and rubbed at the back of his neck. "I haven't been my own boss that long."

"Just long enough to have a second résumé. Which is more than I have, and exactly what I need."

"And so you push."

She rose to pace the floor. "You know as well as I do that some of the businesses on these streets are nothing but toys to the owners. I can't afford to play.

I can't even afford to break even. I've got to make a profit."

"It takes time to get up and running."

"I don't have time." Anxiety filtered into her voice, and into the steps that took her from one side of the room to the other. "My babies' futures depend on whether or not I can make a go of this store, this year. If it doesn't look like it's going to happen"—or if it didn't look like the life she wanted to live—"then it's back to the old résumé and New York."

Jace stepped in her path.

Eden looked up. "What?"

"Babies? As in more than one?"

She nodded. "Twins. Haven't I told you?"

He shook his head, his mouth twitched and then his smile widened. "Two babies? On your own? You are a brave woman, Eden Karr."

She wasn't about to tell him how frightened she was. She wasn't even sure she was ready to admit that to herself. Or to add to her list of uncertainties. "Courage doesn't have a lot to do with it. These just happen to be the cards I've drawn."

His gaze traveled from her gently rounded belly to her eyes. His twinkled when he said, "I'd say you're holding a full house."

Eden refrained from shaking her head. "A stand-up carpenter. I'm so impressed." She leaned back against the frame of the screen door. "Molly's already appointed herself surrogate grandmother. And as handy as you are, I'm sure a surrogate carpenter might be nice to have around."

"I get by with a little help from my friends?"

You are just a fount of cleverness today. But, yes. Something like that."

A change came over Jace. It wasn't an obvious switch in mood, like the ones plaguing her these days. No, this was a subtle shift, more body language than anything. A withdrawal that she hadn't expected.

"I'd like to help, Eden. I really would. But I think you've got the right idea about keeping this relationship business." Almost as if his body ignored the very words he was speaking, he moved forward, slowly, into her space.

His boots gave him two added inches of height. His black T-shirt barely accommodated his shoulders; his black hair was a sleep-mussed mane. And when he reached up and stroked a palm over her hair, Eden's heart lurched in response.

"I don't make a very reliable friend. I think you should know that." He reached behind her and fumbled for the doorknob. Electric air crackled between them. He waited, for a long minute he waited. Then, without another word, he stepped around her and strode outside.

Eden spilled a long rush of breath and watched him leave, realizing once he'd gone—and once she'd regained her solid footing, which had slipped away at his touch—that he'd done it again. Brought up questions she wanted answers to and left her hanging on a curious hook.

Why had he replaced the chime? Why did he run her errands, bring her lunch? Why was a man with his credentials living in a barn in an open pasture? Why would J. B. Morgan refuse to use J. B. Morgan's résumé?

And why did he think he couldn't be her friend . . . when he already was?

John and Annette Philips, proprietors of The Emporium, offered the use of their second floor for Arbor Glen's monthly town meeting. John took pride in the organization of his half of the combination hardware/dry goods/arts-and-crafts store, where many of the local artists shopped for supplies.

Annette's half was as whimsical as John's was precise. Dried herbs and flowers hung suspended from the low ceiling among floating streamers of cornhusk ribbons and lace. The aroma of orange and spice wafted through the air to mingle with lavender and rose.

Glad to find the store deserted, Eden covetously eyeballed a grapevine wreath draped in netting of primary colors, yellow, red, green and blue ribbons hanging from a building block locomotive.

Had Annette been anywhere around, she'd no doubt insist that the wreath was perfect for Eden's nursery. Eden agreed. Her checkbook didn't. She couldn't spend another frivolous penny until she'd tallied the sales from the Spring Fest.

The buzz of conversation reached her ears as she slowly climbed the stairs. Making her way into the room, she chose a folding chair in the back row, turned it sideways and propped her feet in the one beside it. The huge ceiling fan overhead stirred the hair around her face.

She'd barely tucked the strands behind her ear and crossed her ankles in the chair seat before Molly came alongside. The way she clucked her tongue made Eden feel like a tiny yellow, henpecked chick.

Well, not so tiny.

"You're not restin', are you, girl?"

"As a matter of fact, I slept past closing this afternoon." She narrowed one eye in accusation, loving the way Molly always rose to the bait. "And if you'd come back from where you disappeared to instead of leaving Jace in charge of the store, you'd know that."

"My, my, aren't we in a tiff?"

"No. Not a tiff." Eden sighed. "I just had a disagreement with Jace."

"A fight?" Molly's arched brow indicated matchmaking interest. "I didn't know you two were close enough to have anything to fight about."

"It wasn't a fight. It was a difference of opinion." Eden crossed her arms and propped them on her stomach. "And we're not close at all. We're strictly business associates."

"I'm sure you're right." Molly's expression was the picture of innocence. "Why else would he swear me to secrecy and nearly break his neck to put up that new doorchime as a surprise?"

Eden couldn't resist. "And what doorchime would that be?"

"The one you heard when you opened the door this evening."

"Molly Hansen, have you been spying?"

"Of course I have," the older woman admitted without a hint of shame. "I left early so Jace could finish up while you were asleep. Then I kept an eye out from the bakery window. But that lace curtain of yours got in the way and I couldn't see a thing."

"Serves you right." Eden didn't want anyone to see her tears. Even Molly. Besides, Molly's earlier comment deserved further exploration. "He nearly broke his neck, huh?"

"Took a backward step and was inches from coming off that ladder of his." Molly tapped a finger against her chin. "It happened right after I mentioned what a good thing it was that you and he had become such fast friends."

"That would explain his suicide attempt," Eden grumbled beneath her breath.

"What's that?"

"Just remarking on the nature of the beast." Eden propped her left foot on her right thigh and rubbed her swollen ankle.

"What beast? Oh, Jace?" Molly tittered, pressed her fingers to her mouth, tittered again. Then she laid a hand on Eden's arm and whispered, "I promise not to tell a soul."

"Tell a soul what?" Eden took in the older woman's exaggerated wink. "You mean Jace? And me? You've got it all wrong—"

"Yes, dear. I'm sure I do." Another wink. "Now, that beastly Tucker of mine needs me up front. Tomorrow afternoon I'll wake you after two hours. Nothing less. You *will* rest."

Tucker stomped his boot three times in lieu of a gavel and took his position at the end of a picnic table behind the First Baptist Church's old classroom podium. He could barely see over the top. "We need to get started, folks. Molly's got another dozen batches of cookies to bake tonight, and I don't want to be up late sampling them all."

A chorus of good-natured chuckles erupted from the three dozen or so residents as Molly took her seat at Tucker's side. Folding chair legs scraped over the floor, echoing in the huge room. The murmur of voices dulled to a low din. The five permanent council members settled down on the benches.

"John Philips will be talking first." Tucker stepped back and motioned for John to approach the lectern. The talk centered on plans for the Spring Fest. Eden listened with only one ear. Instead she mentally reviewed the figures she'd been working on when she fell asleep that afternoon.

It was time to start thinking about her fall line, as well as what she wanted to stock for Christmas. Getting an advance preview of a season's styles had been a favorite part of the work she'd done at *Elite Woman* magazine. The perk of traveling to designer showings and fashion events was one she would miss— already missed, if she was going to be completely honest.

But she had noticed that her thoughts of late turned less to the past and more to the future. The changes she was making to the shop were a part of that, she knew. Any progress forward tended to

make it an unproductive waste of time to focus on
a former way of life.

And she hadn't left the business altogether. She'd
just brought a piece of New York and the world to
Arbor Glen. Just as Jace had brought his talent and
eye for design of another sort.

Now, why in the middle of thinking of her future
had she thought of Jace? A frisson of awareness
shifted through her and she turned. Hands crossed
over his chest, Jace lounged against the doorjamb
at the top of the stairs. On some peripheral level,
Eden had heard Tucker Hansen pose a question that
Jace was answering.

Of course. That's why she'd thought of him. It was
a natural extension of hearing him speak. What
wasn't natural were the feelings sifting through her,
the connection they shared that had her surfacing
from her subconscious at the sound of his voice.

And then he slid his gaze her way and winked. In
the middle of discussing the running of electrical
power for the Spring Fest, he slid his gaze her way
and winked. Eden flounced back around, facing forward and the dozens of curious glances aimed her
way.

Damn the beast. He'd declared their relationship
strictly business, then flirted with her there in front
of half the town and the First Baptist Church's old
classroom podium. He didn't want to be friends, yet
he was acting like a suitor.

How in the world was she supposed to keep this
relationship strictly business when Jace refused to
practice what he preached?

* * *

At the end of the short walk home from the meeting, Eden found Jace in her kitchen slicing tomatoes while bacon sizzled in a cast-iron skillet. The salty smell of frying pork and the aroma of Molly's toasted home-baked bread set Eden's stomach to growling.

Her gaze swept across the set of Jace's shoulders, then roamed with interest down the tapering line of his back to the firm buttocks and muscled legs that filled his blue jeans with purpose.

Blowing out a long breath of appreciation—for both the smell of the food and the physical perfection of the man—she leaned back against the door frame. "What are you doing here?"

He shrugged but didn't turn, too busy with the knife to look up. "You went to the meeting without eating. You've got to be hungry."

She had. She was. But that he'd noticed and intervened was interesting. Crossing the room, she snatched a strip of crisp bacon from the paper towel on the counter, snapped it in half and popped it in her mouth. "Thanks."

Jace grunted noncommittally, grabbed hot bread from the toaster and dropped the slices on a plate.

Eden waved the other half of the bacon back and forth like a windshield wiper. "Oh, and thanks for giving half the town at least a week's worth of grist for the gossip mill."

"Only a week? I must be losing my touch." He

flipped the bacon and crossed the room to the refrigerator.

Eden leaned back against the counter. The sharp edge of the kitchen counter bit into her back. Tired and confused, she wasn't going to let him blow this off again. "I wouldn't know about whether or not you're losing your touch. Which is probably best, since that's rather personal and we're not really *friends*."

A jar of mayonnaise hit the table with a thud. A bottle of beer followed. Slowly, Jace turned, looking at her over the refrigerator's open door. "Do you really think you want to be friends with me, Eden?"

Eden wanted that at the very least. "Yes. I do."

Shaking his head, Jace crossed the room and tossed a head of lettuce into the sink. He ripped off one leaf after another. Cold drops of water pelted Eden's bare arm. Others popped and sizzled as they landed in the hot skillet.

She bit her tongue and waited.

He slapped the rest of the bacon onto the paper towels, shoved the skillet back off the fire and slung the spatula down hard enough that bacon grease splattered the stovetop in big oily circles. This time, when he turned, nothing about the look in his eyes was playful.

"You're asking for trouble."

"I don't think so."

He took a step closer, scant inches of warm body heat between them, hands braced on lean and sexy hips. "I do."

"Well, you're wrong."

"We're doing fine with a relationship that's business, Eden. Let's just keep things the way they are."

She dropped her gaze to the floor, only to have it wind up on her belly—a belly that except for the width of a breath was touching his. "Your actions speak a lot louder than your words, Jace. Everything you do proves that we've already taken our relationship beyond professional bounds."

He blew out a low, exasperated breath. "You're making more of what I do than you should."

"No. I'm not." She raised her chin, putting her eyes level with the hollow of his throat. She swallowed. Hard. "I could use a friend right now. And I don't believe a word of what you say about not being a good friend to have."

She waited for his decision, her eyes flicking from his back to the hollow of his throat. The pulse there beat visibly. His chest rose and fell, his hands clenched and released.

Finally, he pulled a chair from beneath the table. Leaning both hands on the top rung, he stared down at the seat and exhaled.

SIX

"I can't give you what you need, Eden." Jace shoved the chair up under the table and grabbed the bottle of beer. He took one long swallow, then added, "I don't know what else you want me to say."

Eden's fingers itched to brush the hair back from his forehead, to tunnel through the shaggy waves in back, to jerk his head up and make him look her in the eye.

"I want you to explain to me the dynamics of our relationship. I want to be sure I don't cross any of the lines you've drawn in the sand."

He made his way to the other side of the room and switched off the gas burners. His expression was equal parts weariness and resignation, his eyes a pale blue, lightly smiling, when he met her gaze.

"I guess you won't buy the line about us being business associates."

She blew out a gust of breath. "Sure. Why not? Business associates works for me." He wasn't the only one who was tired. And she had better things on which to expend her energies than this aggravating hardheaded man.

"You know, the more I think about it, Jace, the more I realize that you're right."

"About what?"

"To stick to your guns about being only my carpenter, since it's too tough for you to be my friend."

Jace rubbed his hands over his face, then moved them to his hips and gave in with a quirk of his mouth and a shake of his head. "Okay. We're friends. Are you happy now?"

"No, but it doesn't matter." That was a lie, of course, because it did matter, but she knew he was right in staving off even the casual involvement she was pressing for.

He was the one who was the enigma, the mysterious J. B. Morgan who refused his name, his talent, his past. And here she was pushing, wanting to make of him what he wasn't when she should've been grateful for his honesty.

Hadn't she learned anything from Nate?

She stared at the grouping of antique cookie cutters on the wall behind the table and waited for him to leave. From the corner of her eye she watched him head for the back door, but once there he hooked his fingers in the frame overhead. And instead of leaving, he stared out the square-paned window into the night.

He rubbed one hand over his neck, massaging the muscles bunched there, then turned back to the room. Eden found her gaze drifting down his body dressed all in black, a piratical silhouette against the glossy white paint.

Feelings she'd sworn not to entertain flitted

through parts of her body she'd sworn to ignore. A dull ache pooled deep, heated the skin between her legs with a warmth, a pulsing warmth that was purely sexual and had nothing to do with the pressure brought by carrying twins.

Oh, Lord, she was lost; she was insane, wanting a man who she shouldn't be wanting, a man who was doing his gentle best to let her down. She walked to the table, pulled out a chair and eased down because it was all she could do.

The room echoed still and quiet, and Eden glanced up when Jace moved. He stopped at the stove, picked up a piece of bacon, snapped it in half and crumbled it in his hand.

Wiping his greasy palm on his jeans, he leaned back against the counter. "You remember the friend with the wife who liked hats?" he asked, talking down to his feet.

"The hat rack. Sure." Interesting opening statement. "Terri, right?"

"Right. Well, Terri is Kevin's wife."

"And you and Kevin were friends."

"Yeah. Past tense." He bit off a laugh. "That's probably how Kevin feels, anyway."

Jace returned to the back door. This time he opened it. A soft spring breeze drifted through the screen, bringing a hint of honeysuckle and mimosa inside. The room hummed with expectancy and Eden found herself holding her breath.

"I've known Kevin since junior high," Jace said. "We went to different schools before that but hooked up the minute we hit sixth grade. Robert and Jimmy Marvin moved into the district during the middle of seventh grade.

"The four of us went through the next six years like one brain, one body with eight legs. One got sick, we all got sick. One decided to play soccer instead of football, we all played soccer instead of football.

"Marv found his older brother's stash of girlie mags and developed an interest in women, so we all . . . well, you get the picture."

Jace pushed on the screen door frame, testing the strength of the flimsy hook latch Eden had screwed in herself. "Thing is, it didn't stop there."

"College?" Eden asked, saying as little as possible and hoping what she chose to say would be just leading enough to encourage Jace to reveal more.

He nodded, shrugged, a slow roll easing tense muscles, then let his shoulders droop. "Texas A & M. Thing is, as close as we were, we'd all been each other's worst nightmare when it came to competition.

"And once we got to college, the race took on a whole new meaning. We joked around about it, making bets; small ones at first, but then the rivalry grew fangs."

His expression grew closed and solemn. "It wasn't fun anymore."

It was so hard not to press when she wanted to do just that. But if she didn't let Jace tell this his way, he might not tell it at all. "What happened?"

He rolled his eyes, expelled a snort of breath. "We shot to the tops of our individual fields, earned a hell of a lot of money and achieved a professional regard unheard of for anyone our age."

"And this was a bad thing?"

"Not at first," he said, shaking his head. "But it got to the point that nothing else mattered but beating the pants off each other. And even lifelong friendships can't stand that sort of battering for long."

"No, but friendships do change over the years." Even she hadn't kept in contact with the friends she'd left behind in New York, and she'd only been gone four months. "Careers and family can take you in different directions. You drift apart, lose touch."

"And that's okay, as long as you keep them on your Christmas card list, right?"

The rapid tic in his jaw made Eden catch her breath. This was about way more than Christmas cards. "Well . . . I suppose that's not the ideal solution. But it does happen."

Jace crossed the room and pulled out a chair from beneath the table, turning it so that when he sat his knees, though they didn't touch, bracketed hers. "It shouldn't happen. Not when the friends in question have been a major, a *daily* part of your life for fifteen years."

He picked a piece of lint from the knee of her navy leggings. "Here's the thing, Eden. I don't even have an address for Robert or Marv. Kevin's in Colorado. Aurora, I think.

"And these are the friends who quit the team when I got cut from soccer in eighth grade, who skipped the prom, picked up pizza and hung out at my house because I'd broken my hip two weeks before.

"These guys have always been there for me. They came to the Farriday dedication to celebrate my success. But I wasn't there for any of them. Not when Robert made partner in his law firm. Not when Kevin and Terri got married.

"Not even when Marv suffered a heart attack." Jace leaned his elbows on his thighs and buried his face in his hands. "A heart attack, for crying out loud. And he was only in his early thirties."

"And you feel guilty about that, don't you? Not that you weren't there," she went on to explain when he looked up and she sensed he was ready to interrupt. "But that he had the heart attack in the first place? That a friendly rivalry was the cause?"

"Not the cause, but definitely a contributing factor. The competition was my idea. The result of a lot of beer and a lot of bragging during a Spring Break keg party our senior year at A & M. Thing is, even after we sobered up, we were stupid enough to go ahead with it."

A grim smile twisted his mouth. "And the rivalry wasn't so friendly."

Eden heard the regret in his voice, saw it in his eyes. Hated that he was holding himself singularly responsible for the decision of four. "And how would things have been different if you hadn't gone ahead with this competition?

"Obviously, you were all incredibly driven, incredibly talented. Do you think that you—that any of you—would've pushed yourselves any less?"

"I think we might've done more pulling together and left the cutthroat tactics for the sharks," he said and slumped back in his chair.

"You said the others came to the Farriday dedication." She smiled, looking for good news where she could. "That sounds to me like they were pulling for you."

"But I never pulled for them. Which is something I have to deal with. And why, even though you and I have a relationship that's gone beyond business," he reluctantly admitted with a smile, "I can't be the friend you need. Not when I have this history of failing those closest to me."

She heard him. She didn't believe him. She wanted to smack some sense into him. What good were isolation and withdrawal when all this time later he still shouldered blame?

He could hardly spend the rest of his life living like a hermit, unsure how his friends felt about his defection, unsure what had become of them, where they were, how life had touched them, when he would see them again . . . and why should he, when the phone was but an arm's length away?

And then she remembered the rest of what he'd said, words about failing those closest to him. Tentatively reaching for one of his hands, she asked, "Jace? Am I close to you?"

He laughed low in his throat. "Probably too close."

She pressed. "And that bothers you?"

"Only a lot." He squeezed her hand, twining his fingers through hers. "But what bothers me the most is that I slaved over a hot stove and now the bacon's probably cold."

"That's okay," she said, ready to let him off the hook. Neither of them needed to take this any farther tonight, if they needed to take it farther at all. "I don't have much of an appetite."

Jace grinned his cocky devil's grin, a smile that slid over her like sexy silk undies and almost took her apart. "Well, now. You not having an appetite has to be a first."

"If I wasn't so tired I'd hurt you for that." She forced a small yawn, wanting him to go because suddenly she wanted him to stay. "I think I'll make it an early night. The Festival starts Tuesday, and I've got a lot to do tomorrow."

"Right. And I need to finish up the shelves so I can get started in the kitchen next week. Your new cabinets are splitting the seams of my workroom." He touched her cheek in farewell, started to get to his feet and stopped.

Like an unexpected change of heart, indecision flickered in his eyes. His fingers slid to her nape. His thumb pressed the manic pulse in her throat. His eyes narrowed, his black-fringed gaze a sultry mix of wonder and want.

Jace pulled. Eden closed her eyes and followed.

Warm breath fanned her cheek. His lips brushed hers. Breathless, delicate kisses, the barest touch of mouth on mouth. Nibbling, teasing, nuzzling, so soft.

She opened her mouth under his and tasted, the salt of bacon and man. Teased, her lips nipping at his, her mouth pressing hard. Tempted, her palm splayed flat on his heartbeat and up, sliding to the slope of his jaw and into his hair.

Jace responded like a man, sliding forward on his chair, almost into hers. He swallowed her kiss with a hunger that trembled beneath her touch. "Christ, Eden. Touch me."

Enticed to madness, Eden laid her hands on his thighs. The taut muscles jumped beneath her fingertips. She slipped her palms higher, to his hips, holding him the way he held her. Like she'd die if she didn't.

Time stood still. The hour, the minute, seconds disappeared. Nothing mattered. Only Jace, the way his mouth fed on hers, the way his five o'clock shadow abraded the skin from her jaw to her ear.

He nipped the lobe, breathing sweet words, trailing intimate sounds to her throat. She shivered, shuddered, spun like ribbons of gold in the sun.

Whimpers of need spilled from her lips, and Jace's groan was gut-level deep. His fingers fumbled with the buttons at her neck, then lower and lower still.

Air breathed over her throat, her collarbone, the swell of one breast. Jace's mouth followed, tracing a path to the cleft of her breasts. Her skin tingled, her breathing ached, her nipples pleaded for his touch.

She tossed her head back, invited him close and, for the first time in months, let herself feel. Oh, she'd forgotten what it felt like to feel.

Her palms slid under his shirt, up his back, soothing tense muscles, testing resilient skin and strength held in check. Her ivory linen blouse gaped open to the lace of her bra, and the silk of his hair rubbed friction and fire on her skin.

He gripped her upper arms, slid his fingers beneath the bra straps, working them down. His tongue performed wickedness in the hollow of her throat, down the center of her chest, wetting the edge of the lace covering her full breasts.

And then he stopped, stiffened, slumped back in his chair. Fever brightness burned in his eyes. The cords in his neck stood in rigid relief.

Muscles bunched beneath his black shirt. Urgency swirled thick through the air and even thicker beneath Jace's jeans, ten washings past worn.

Refusing to look away, Eden reached for her clothes. She damned herself for recklessly surrendering to physical passion. She *knew* better. Knew where her priorities lay. And sex was nowhere on the list.

Jace brushed her hands aside and gently straightened the straps of her bra. Starting at the top, he buttoned her buttons. And then he raised his head.

His voice rumbled low and deep, husky with lust—and regret—when he said, "Do you really think that we can be friends? With this thing between us?"

She knew he was right, but it didn't ease the ache. Chin up, she stood. He got to his feet as well and, without giving her a chance to say a word, ran one finger across her cheek. He raked back his hair, scrubbed both hands down his face.

Then he turned and walked into the night.

* * *

He hadn't meant to kiss her. He really hadn't. And now he damn sure wished that kiss had never happened, because he could think of nothing else.

The big white bandage swathing his left thumb proved the point. He hadn't missed with a hammer in years.

Four days ago, the morning after their ill-fated showdown, he'd purposefully delayed his arrival until noon, counting on the fact that, if she'd stuck to her usual timetable, Eden would be busy in the shop.

After skulking through the back door into the kitchen, he'd spent the day boxing up the contents of her two kitchen cabinets before tearing them down from the wall. The mindless labor gave him too much time to think, and his imagination took over where the kiss left off.

Seconds into picturing Eden naked and stretched out on his bed, he'd brought the hammer down on his thumb, effectively derailing his train of thought, as well as a good day's work.

Friday morning he'd shown up minutes after she opened shop and worked like a madman to finish dismantling and hauling away the debris before she closed The Fig Leaf at five.

The worst part of those few days had been passing her in the hallway, or running into her in the kitchen, with nothing more than a mumbled, "Hi." That, and the meals he'd eaten alone.

He'd sat on the tailgate of his truck and chewed a tasteless ham and cheese sandwich, thinking of the reasons he'd moved to Arbor Glen, reasons he'd done a good job of sitting on until, with Eden's simply asked questions, he'd opened a vein and bled out his past.

And until he'd been stupid enough to kiss her.

Feeling her warm lips pressed against his had been the purest kind of torture. But a different kind of torture than forcing her to understand who and what he was.

He hadn't wanted sympathy. Or pity. And neither was what she'd offered. What she wanted to give him he couldn't take without hating himself for the rest of his life.

He and Eden had no future. She was a determined single woman, making a life for herself and her unborn children. And that life might one day take her back into the jaws of the very monster that had wreaked havoc on Jace's life.

He wasn't about to confront the demon on its own feeding grounds. Yeah, he was afraid. He knew the lure of success, the high that came with celebrity, with every professional coup.

Knew, too, that avoiding temptation was the surest way to guarantee that he wouldn't fall back into those old traps. And avoiding temptation meant keeping his distance from the woman who could take him there.

Right now he wasn't able to completely understand what he felt for Eden. Their relationship had gone way past business and, though it pained him to admit it, way past friendship. He owed her an apology for walking out the way he had. "I'm sorry" didn't seem like enough.

This first day of the Spring Fest seemed busy. Even at nine o'clock this morning, he'd barely been able to pull into the traffic on Highway 37.

Halfway down Main he'd nailed his brakes to the floor to avoid hitting a kid running across the street in front of his truck.

His heart still pounding from the near miss, he'd pulled to a stop in her drive, grinding his gears as he searched for neutral. He'd climbed from the truck and walked through her back door into the kitchen just as she'd pushed away from her breakfast.

Their "Good mornings" had come on top of each other, the atmosphere strained, uncomfortable; they were strangers who knew more than strangers should. At least the day was almost over.

Catching the corner of the screen with the heel of his boot, he maneuvered through her back door, hauling in the last of the new cabinets. And came face-to-face with Chloe Angelino.

Face to foot seemed more accurate. She sat yoga style. On top of his six-foot ladder. Her bare feet soles up in the bend of her knees.

Paint splatters dotted her long bare legs and the sleeves of the flannel shirt she'd knotted at her midriff. Her shorts were too short, to Jace's way of thinking.

From his vantage point, leg wasn't all he could see. "Can't you read?"

She lowered her gaze from the ceiling to his face. "When I find it necessary."

He stacked the cabinets on top of one another,

crossed the room and jabbed at the sticker on the top step with one finger. DO NOT STAND ON OR ABOVE THIS STEP. YOU CAN LOSE YOUR BALANCE.

"I never lose my balance," Chloe said with a toss of her head.

"There's a first time for everything." Jace held on to the sides. "I'd rather not be around for yours. Down. Now."

Chloe expelled a long breath and Jace looked away as she descended rump first.

"I hope you haven't tracked paint through the house," he said, noting the rainbow of primary colors she wore.

Chloe tightened the knot that held her shirt together, propped her hands on her hips and glared at Jace beneath a fluff of teenage bangs. "You sound just like a father."

He forgave her everything in that instant. "You'd know better than I."

"Well, you do. And don't worry. There is not a drop of paint anywhere I did not purposefully put it."

"Including yourself?"

"Of course. I have to check the mixtures in natural light."

"So you slap a paintbrush on your body?"

"No. I test various color combinations until I get the shade I need."

"And when you find it, then you connect the dots, right?" Jace nodded toward her legs, then moved the ladder to the section of wall where he planned to hang the first cabinet.

Toes pointed, Chloe balanced one heel on the lip of the sink and examined her spotted leg from all angles. "Art is a very individual form of expression. I don't expect you to understand."

"Don't worry. I'm not going to try." He climbed on the countertop, level in hand, pencil behind his ear. "So what're you doing down here?"

"Checking on your progress."

"Any particular reason?" He glanced back over his shoulder.

Sitting on the edge of the sink, Chloe turned the water to warm. "I'll be painting the kitchen when you're done."

"With any luck, and no more interruptions, I'll be finished today," Jace replied, eyeballing the bubble in the level.

"Why don't you like me, Jace Morgan?"

Her tiny voice cut to the quick. With a deep sigh, he laid the level atop the fridge and dropped to his haunches on the countertop. Wrists draped on his knees, he watched Chloe wash her legs in the kitchen sink with Ivory soap.

"I *do* like you, Chloe. I just forget my manners sometimes."

"Your mother must not have taught you well."

"She tried. I didn't listen."

"Neither did I."

He felt it again, that kinship, that strange, burning, electric connection. Her eyes hypnotized. His breathing slowed and Jace decided he'd definitely been living in the woods too long. "So, what do you have planned for the kitchen?"

"White, of course, because of its purity. Then sten-
cils in blues and greens. I can't decide on the rose.
I don't know if it goes with Eden's skin."

"Apricot," Jace said without thinking.

"Yes. Apricot. I'd even thought of peach, but apricot has the perfect blush." She narrowed one eye
and looked right through the wall he'd thrown up
when he realized his mistake. "You now know Eden
better than I."

Jace hopped off the counter, threw Chloe a towel
from the stack folded on the kitchen table and made
easy work of carrying the first cabinet across the
room. "You're the artist. And Eden trusts you. You
decide."

Chloe stepped into his path as he turned to go
back for the second. "You decided for me. And if
you had any manners at all, you would apologize for
lying to yourself."

"About what?" Jace forced a suspicious scowl.

"About Eden, of course."

Dead on again, kid. Dead on again. He walked
around her and hefted the second cabinet up off
the floor. "So, did the frame work out?"

"Yes. Stone Healen fixed the glass. I have all the
drawings framed but one."

"Why's that?"

"There is a piece missing. A piece I cannot find."

"You need help looking?"

She reached for the knot on her shirt. "It is here,
deep inside."

"Never mind." He set the cabinet next to the first
and, before he could take another step, Chloe's

arms came around his waist from the back. She squeezed.

"The frame is perfect. And you are wonderful. Thank you, Jace Morgan. I'm glad that you're my friend."

"You're welcome and . . . me, too." His voice sounded strangled and strange and he stiffened, waiting for distant memories to dispel the warmth of Chloe's innocent touch. Nothing happened.

All he felt was joy, and a growing affection for this kid who was like no one he'd ever known. Before he could figure out how to untangle himself from her tight hug, she disappeared into the shop, only to return seconds later.

Her eyes were comic-book round and wide when she said, "Eden needs you."

Jace frowned, surprised that after the past several days she'd need him for anything. "Okay. Sure."

When he walked through into the shop it was like stepping from a sauna into frigid winter air. Tension hung in the room, darkening the carnival mood of the Festival.

He scanned the shop, lighting at last on Eden's profile, knowing her agitated state was what he'd picked up on.

She sat at the counter, her back rigid, her leaf-green eyes wide, her lower lip caught between her teeth. Customers milled the aisles. But Eden had eyes for only one couple.

He walked up behind her and whispered, "You okay?"

She jumped, looked his way with a distracted smile

and gave a quick, jerky nod. "I'm fine," she answered, and turned back to ring up another sale.

Jace used the time to study the couple who'd so captivated her attention. Both were attractive, their fit-as-a-dollar-can-buy physiques the epitome of yuppie chic.

Not a hair strayed out of place on their casually styled blond heads. Even his gold watch and her diamond earrings were deceptively understated.

What was going on here? Jace moved to stand behind Eden's stool and propped one foot on the lowest rung. Her tension ebbed a fraction as he laid a hand at the small of her back, giving her support for what the hell he had no idea.

SEVEN

"Are you okay?" Her tension seeped into his body through the palm he held pressed to her rigid spine.

"I'm fine. Really." She smiled at him over her shoulder. "But could you stay here? For a minute?"

"Sure. Not a problem." He leaned against the wall behind her and moved his hand to her shoulder. And he ignored the sudden double-time of his heart when she linked two of her fingers through two of his and moved his hand to her hip.

"Do you know them?" he asked, because whatever was going on with her had to do with the couple in question.

"No. Funny. But I thought I did." She released his hand then and turned to ring up a customer.

Thinking she did had obviously been what set her off. Her frazzled nerves were evident in her stiff stance, her shaking hands. He wanted to take her by the elbow and usher her upstairs, get her out of here and give her a chance to breathe. But he knew she wasn't about to leave the store even if he offered to stay.

The next second the cavalry charged through the

door. A flurry of energy, Molly Hansen breezed her way to the counter and shook a stern finger at Jace. "You'd best wipe that scowl off your face, Jace Morgan. Eden doesn't need you to be driving away her customers."

No. Eden needed something else. Molly's admonition registered in the only corner of his mind not focused on Eden. It was a very small corner. He drew Molly aside. "Molly, do me a favor."

"Only if you stop scowling."

Smiling weakly, he cast a covert glance at Eden. She rang up the same sale three times before getting it right. Shaking his head, he brought his gaze back to Molly. "Can you watch the shop for the last hour? Eden's dead on her feet."

Molly swept a concerned gaze over Eden and headed that way, clicking her tongue in a quick tsk-tsk. Like a junior Schwartzkopf, she took over by storm, coddling Eden with one arm draped across her shoulder.

"You hie yourself on up to bed, you hear? I'm finishing out the day for you."

"I can't ask you to do that," Eden argued, though Jace read the want-to in her eyes.

"No one's asking. I'm insisting. Think of those depending on you." With a steady pressure, she guided Eden to the stairs. "You look to be on your last leg."

Eden's gaze flicked from the register to the milling customers. She shook her head. "No. I'm fine. Really. You and Jace both worry too much."

She took a determined step toward the register

and snagged one foot on the edge of a braided rag
rug. Arms flailing, she stumbled forward toward the
counter, a slow-motion disaster unfolding.

Jace sprang forward, hooked his hands beneath
her arms and dragged her back against his body.
Long seconds later, seconds spent separating their
heartbeats, seconds spent steadying Eden while his
emotional balance tumbled away, he let her go.

She pushed a fall of hair from her face and gave
him a feeble smile. "My hero."

"Eden, if you don't take a care now, the next few
months will be the death of you." Molly narrowed
tender, caring and insistent eyes Eden's way.

Eden sighed, looked from Jace to Molly. "Are you
sure?"

"Of course I'm sure. Now scoot," Molly ordered,
sending her on her way with a pat on the bottom.
She waved Jace away as well, ordering him to follow
with no more than a frown.

He hung around long enough for Molly to settle
in before heading for the stairs. Taking them two at
a time, he scaled the distance from the first floor
into the privacy of Eden's rooms. He'd never been
above the first floor and felt like an intruder.

The floorboards creaked beneath his weight as he
made his way down the hall. A rectangle of light
shone from the room at the end. Even before reaching it, he knew it would be the nursery. He stopped
at the door, silently debating his next move.

Eden sat in the windowseat, running one index
finger down a single square pane, the screeching
noise reflecting her distress. "You don't have to hide

in the hall, Morgan. I'm not going to bite your head off. Or dissolve into a puddle of tears."

Jace exhaled long and slow. "That's good to hear. Either one would make quite a mess and I don't have a mop on me."

She glanced over her shoulder, a lopsided attempt at a grin almost reaching her eyes before she turned her attention to the limb of a pecan tree bobbing against the window.

And then she sighed. "Has there been anyone in your life you never wanted to see again? Thought you'd never see again? But you look up and there he is? Standing right in front of you?"

He took a tentative step into the room. "So that's what that was about. The couple in the shop. You thought it was your ex?"

Eden leaned her forehead against the glass, her reflected image a study in dejection. "The resemblance was amazing. Though it's hard to think of him as my ex, when he was never really my current."

"I'd wondered about that. Not that it was any of my business—"

"But you wondered anyway," she said and smiled.

"Sure. I mean, you're five months pregnant. Alone. And you have been for quite a while. I figure that whatever happened with your breakup, it had to do with the pregnancy." He eased his weight down to the top of a wooden toy chest, taking as much care as he gently settled as he had with his words.

"It did. But in a very convoluted way."

"I'm guessing you weren't married?"

"No. I would've married him. In fact, I proposed to him."

Why did his heart lurch at that? "And he said no?"

She turned on the windowseat and leaned back against the glass. "It was after I found out that I was pregnant. Nate—that was his name. Nate and I had never talked of starting a family. Or of getting married. But he was a good man.

"We'd been together three years. And even though the pregnancy was an accident, I thought, you know, maybe this is a sign that it's time to do something permanent with this relationship."

"You loved him?"

"I did." She nodded, shrugged. "Oh, he probably wasn't the great passion of my life, but we were very comfortable together. I did a lot of traveling. And it was always nice to know he'd be there when I got home.

"He practiced law. In Manhattan. We were both so busy that the time we had together was spent enjoying the present. We never talked about the future."

"Until you got pregnant." Elbows on his knees, he steepled his fingers under his chin and waited.

"I set the whole romantic stage. The candles. The firelight. The music. I told him we were going to have a baby. I asked him to marry me." A laugh, dry and brittle, erupted from her throat. "And that's when he told me he was already married. That he'd been married for eleven years."

Jace tightened his gut against the hot poker

scorching a hole from his belly to his back. "What a bastard."

Slowly she scooted around on the seat, lowered her feet to the floor and clutched the cushion at her sides. "The next four weeks were a whirlwind while I decided what to do. I wanted the baby more than anything. But I knew that my career wasn't conducive to raising a child.

"If I'd had a husband, it would've been different. But I didn't. And if I'd stayed at the magazine, I would've needed a nanny and a housekeeper, and they would've been the ones raising my child. But that wasn't what I wanted."

"And so the career change."

"Exactly. How to combine my profession with single parenting? My father raised me alone." She smiled, as if the memory brought her comfort. "And I can't imagine growing up in a more loving home. But that's the thing. He *was* home. For dinner every night, for homework. He was also at every fair and exhibition where I showed my designs. And he made sure everyone knew I was his daughter."

She struggled to her feet, fists bolstering the small of her back. "I thought a lot about that. About growing up in a small town. I knew the pace would be slower. I knew it would give me more time with the baby. I didn't know I was having *babies* until after I'd moved."

"But?" Jace asked, knowing there was a big one hanging in the air.

"But it wasn't the life I wanted to live." She lifted a brow, met his gaze head on.

"And now?"

"I'm adjusting. And it's getting easier. But I do miss New York."

"You think you'll go back?"

"One day. Maybe. I'll have to wait and see how things go with The Fig Leaf. And with the twins." She pushed back her hair from her face and stepped closer. "Right now, though, only one thing matters."

Jace looked up. "What's that?"

"Food. I'm starving."

A cleansing sort of laughter erupted deep in his soul, and he bowed his head only to have it land on her stomach. Both froze for the timeless second it took him to make up his mind.

He raised his head a few inches, far enough and long enough to replace his forehead with his hands, molding his palms to her taut form.

"It's absolutely amazing that two people are in there." Jace cleared his throat. Twice. "Lives dependent on you for survival."

Eden laid trembling hands over his. "It's enough to scare the spit out of me."

He felt her fear in her voice and her hands. "Hey, you only have to be a first-time parent once."

"Oh, well, that really helps." A crooked but bona fide smile doused the despondency in her eyes.

He answered with a relieved grin of his own. "My degree's in architecture, not psychology."

"You do okay, doctor."

"Remind me to send you a bill," Jace said just as he felt a quick kick centered midpalm. Another followed close behind. Incredulity spawned his wide-eyed question: "Did you feel that?"

"I feel it twenty-four hours a day. Right now I think someone's telling me they're hungry."

He slapped his palms on his thighs. "Then let's go."

"Where?" She stepped back, giving him room enough to stand.

"Tonight *I'm* going to feed *you.*"

"I hate to tell you this, Morgan, but you've eaten me out of house and home. There's nothing downstairs but oatmeal, eggs and milk, and I'm in no mood to grocery shop."

"Who said anything about shopping? Or eating here, for that matter?"

"You're taking me out?" At his nod, her eyes dimmed like a flickering bulb. "I can't go anywhere looking like this."

"Like what?" He'd never understand women.

Eden pouted. "I'm fat, frazzled and frumpy."

Jace's sigh settled around them with a patience usually spent on hard-to-plane boards. "The frazzled is why I'm taking you out. The fat is baby, not you. The frumpy?"

He poured every ounce of his serious-as-a-heart-attack attraction down the length of her body. He hoped it was enough to dispel her lingering doubts because he was taking a big leap beyond the bounds of the friendship he'd swore to keep casual.

"If frumpy means I want to pull you under me, belly or no, and show you just what our bodies were meant for, then, woman, you've got a major case."

"Oh, God, Jace. Don't tease me."

Jace slid his hands along her waist and pulled her round front against his flat belly as tight as geometry would allow. "Who's teasing?"

She leaned back and fixed him with a wild-eyed look, one that told him all he needed to know about how close she was to falling off an emotional precipice.

"Then why did you kiss me like you meant it, then walk away like I was nothing?" Eden closed her eyes, wanting to bite her tongue even more than she wanted an honest answer. Hugging herself tightly, she walked to the window, searching for serenity in the expansive view outside.

"What's wrong?"

"Nothing," she whispered and shook her head, wishing he'd go away. She'd opened a Pandora's box that she should've padlocked weeks ago.

He took a step closer, the tread of his steps echoing in the nearly empty room. "Ah. Nothing. The word of the day."

"Never mind." She closed her eyes but found the lack of sight heightened other senses. The lightest trace of Chloe's perfume mixed with baby powder, floor wax and paint. It should have been enough to mask the scent of Jace.

Eden peered through the window and focused on a single bud sprouting from the pecan tree limb six inches from the glass. Safe and simple, one step at a time. "I don't want to talk about it."

"Talk about what?"

"You. Me. Everything." She grimaced. Biting her tongue wasn't enough. She needed a chain saw.

"Is that what this is about? You and me?"

His voice came inches from her ear. His fingers settled on her shoulder, the touch gentle, light and so very welcome.

Eden jerked away. There was no "you and me." No matter how hard she might wish it. "I said I don't want to talk about it."

From the corner of her eye, she saw him rake his hair back in frustration, then settle his hands on the waist of his low-riding jeans. "No way, Eden. You always want to talk."

"Not this time."

He moved in, the hunter for the kill. "You want to talk about Chloe's problems, my problems. Now maybe we'd better talk about yours."

She lifted her chin. "I don't have a problem."

"Wrong. You have a big one. We both have a big one."

"When did I become your business?" She sounded incredibly bitchy, but she didn't care. She wanted him to leave. Now. "And when did you become part of any problem I might have?"

"When you insisted we become friends. And the minute you linked you and me together."

"The link was unintentional, believe me." She made a sound of disgust, one designed to drive him away.

"Good. I wouldn't want there to be any mistake."

"The only mistake that's been made here was

when I let you and Molly run me upstairs." She took a retreating step. "I'm going back to the shop."

"Eden, Molly has everything under control. If another crisis comes up, she knows where to find you."

"Crisis? What crisis?" Now she sounded like a hysterical old woman. Why wouldn't he just go away?

"Tell me the truth, Eden. Is being reminded of your ex what's got you upset?" Jace fingered a lock of her hair. "Or is it the fact that I kissed you?"

She pulled her hair from his hand. "Neither one. And I told you, I don't want to talk about it."

He placed a forceful hand on each shoulder and spun her around. She refused to look up. But when she looked down, all she saw were the differences in their bodies, the differences that would always keep them apart.

"That night, Eden. When I kissed you. Did you want me to stay? Did you want me to bring you upstairs, slip off the rest of your clothes and slide my body inside yours? Is that what you wanted?"

His words seduced her, making it hard to tell which would get her into more trouble, the truth or a lie? He took a deep breath, his stomach stroking hers. He slid his hands from her shoulders to her neck and caressed her throat with the pads of his thumbs. She swallowed hard, needing his touch more than air to breathe and hating herself for the weakness.

He lifted her chin with his fist. "That night you needed a friend. Did you want me as a lover, too? I can be one or the other. I can't be both. You want me to scratch your itch?" He arched one wicked brow. "Fine. Let's go do it. But don't expect any more out of the deal."

She steadfastly met his gaze. He'd banked the fire in his eyes, but renegade sparks flickered just the same. She'd have taken him for her lover in an instant, if the act wouldn't destroy her only true friendship.

"I haven't had a friend in a long time, Eden. What we've started building here, I think I really need. And I never would've realized it if you hadn't pushed the way you did." He leaned forward. His cool, dry lips brushed her brow. "Just don't push me any harder. Because I'm damn sure about ready to take whatever else you'll offer."

He let her go then, and walked to the door. With his hand on the knob, he stopped. "I'll be back at six. I owe the three of you a dinner. And friends don't go back on their word."

Eden waited until she heard Jace hit the bottom stair before leaving the nursery. Chloe had made spectacular progress on the mural. The fairies and elves and magical winged creatures possessed such life, Eden wanted to cast off her world for the one portrayed on the wall. Maybe there her restless mind could find answers.

She stopped in the open living area at the top of the stairs and brushed her fingertips over the frame of her loom. When he finally got to talking, Jace just didn't know when to shut up. But she knew he was right. There couldn't be anything but friendship between them. And wasn't that what she wanted?

A friend? A willing ear? Yes, Jace had heard. He'd even listened. But somewhere between kitchen cabinets and their kiss, she'd started thinking of him as more. A dangerous line of thought when she considered that neither one of them wanted involvement.

In the bathroom she pulled aside the shower curtain of blossoms and ferns and turned the faucet to hot. With a splash of bath oil, the scent of apricots bloomed in the air. Eden stripped, then turned and stared at her reflection in the mirror mounted on the back of the door.

What did Jace see when he looked at her? True, at this moment, she resembled a cow. A small cow. But her legs were still trim. She'd only put on about ten pounds, and Lord knew most of that had to be babies. And she'd definitely have a bustline to die for when she was through with all this.

She caressed her collarbone, ran one finger over the swell of a breast and remembered the contrast of Jace's dark head against ivory lace and skin. Shivering with sensation, she climbed into the tub, hoping to wash away his feel, hoping to lose his scent in the steam. Neither happened. Jace was permanently imprinted on all of her senses.

Chin high in the bubbles, she propped her toes on the end of the tub. Water sluiced over her and lapped at her skin while she measured the mound of her belly with her palms.

What would it be like to carry Jace's child? To

witness the wonder she'd seen in his eyes and know he'd had a part in creating this life? What would it be like to love him? To take him inside her body? To become one with a man she wanted the way she wanted Jace?

Soapy water slid over her body like a lover's caress, sweeping a silken path between her legs. Why was she torturing herself with this erotic fantasy? Jace had made his views on life perfectly clear. He intended to remain her friend and nothing more. He wanted no part of her family.

Benjamin and Bethany were her number one priority. And like she'd told Chloe, sex was wonderful. But not without commitment. And not without responsibility. Jace wanted neither. So why did the thought of his touch play such wicked games in her imagination?

Why did she fantasize about sliding her hands through the dark hair on his chest? Lying beneath him, feeling the muscles in his thighs tighten against hers. Urging him deep inside her body. Aching for release.

Simple. She had the hots for Jace Morgan. But she wasn't going to do a damned thing about it. She'd go to dinner with her friend, spend a quiet evening with her friend, and when her friend finished his job, she never wanted to see him again.

With that firm resolve in place, she hit the cold tap with her big toe and froze Jace Morgan out of her mind.

* * *

When Jace got to her house it was still light enough that anyone could see him. He pulled way back in her drive and parked his black Silverado as close to her garage as he could. Why he was being so secretive he wasn't quite sure. But he didn't plan to make a habit of dressing for a date, so he really preferred to keep it between him and Eden.

After tonight, he planned to finish his job and then get back to the life he found so comfortable, the life he shared with no one but Chelsea and her six pups.

Eden'd had a hell of a day. Kind of like the one that broadsided him when he realized how much he meant what he said. He wanted to pull her under him and show her what their bodies were made for. But that wouldn't do much except relieve tension. And he could take care of that alone. With an ax and a log.

He crossed the yard, new grass crunching beneath his feet, and looked up to see her standing on the back porch. Her hair fell to her shoulders in an auburn cloud. Blue flowers trimmed the tiny white collar buttoned at her throat and decorated the hem of the elbow-length sleeves. Her jumper hung loose, the dark fabric of blues and greens moving with the gentle breeze. Her shoes were flat, black, the kind ballet dancers wore.

She looked like a schoolgirl waiting for the bus, except for the barest bulge of her stomach that showed just how much a woman she was. That, and the too-appreciative look in her eyes as she gave him a totally female once-over.

"Excuse me. You must have the wrong house. I'm waiting for my carpenter. He wears jeans and T-shirts."

He'd pulled on a pair of charcoal gray slacks and a black dress shirt but balked at the idea of a jacket and tie. His weight seemed to have rearranged over the last three years, so the waistband rode low on his hips while the fabric clung snugly to his thighs.

Of course, the slacks weren't really meant to be worn with black moccasins, but these were the only shoes he had that weren't covered with a dozen shades of stain.

He propped his hands at his waist. "I thought carpenters wore those pants with loops and tools hanging everywhere."

"That's what I thought, too. A long time ago. But I was wrong."

He stopped in front of her and wondered what else she'd been wrong about. "You still up for this?"

The scent of apricots reached his nose as she stepped down.

"Yeah, we're starving."

He stopped short of telling her that this evening would end the same way it was beginning. On her porch. "Let's go."

He started to take her hand, to guide her across the rough patches of grass, the random clumps of bluebonnets sprouting in her yard, but he shoved his fists in his slacks pockets instead. He couldn't touch her without remembering the taste of her skin. And that wouldn't help his resolve to remain friends. He opened the passenger door of the short wheel-based, step-side pickup.

"You've surprised me again, Morgan." Eden settled into the leather captain's chair and turned her heart-stopping grin his way. "I didn't know you had this much class in you."

He slammed the door on the tailend of Eden's giggle, walked around and climbed into his seat, wondering how long it would take to get her smell out of his truck. Then he wondered if he wanted to. Then he wondered why he was being so stupid.

And why he'd seemed to be that way since he'd met the woman.

EIGHT

The Log Cabin offered Farmersville's fanciest dining. The menu listed standard down-home favorites such as Mom's meatloaf, fried chicken and ham hocks with greens.

Eden had splurged on the chicken-fried steak, mashed potatoes and cream gravy and was absolutely stuffed.

"You want dessert?" Jace asked

"I don't know where I'd put it." She glanced from her half-empty plate to his. "I didn't even finish what I had. I can't believe the portions they serve. Do you want a doggie bag for Chelsea?"

Jace grinned, pulling another fresh yeast roll in half. "Forget Chelsea. How 'bout a doggie bag for me?"

"Now that would be a people bag, and I'm sure you'd have to share anyway."

"You're right about that."

Eden answered his smile. "I guess Chelsea's a lot of company to you."

He seemed to consider, then nodded as he buttered the roll. "She hangs around more now that she's got the pups. And she lets me know if anyone shows up unannounced. Especially at night. I think she's losing her edge, though."

Eden propped her elbows on the table and rested her chin in her palms. "Why's that?"

"She hasn't had much practice. No one comes around but you." Eyes sparkling, he popped the roll half into his mouth.

"No one?"

He shook his head. Swallowed. "Nope. No one."

"Well, I think you need to do something about that."

"Oh, yeah?" He leaned back in his chair, crossed his arms and arched a brow. "Such as?"

"Oh, I don't know. Maybe pick up the phone? Dial Information?" She ran a finger around the rim of her iced-tea glass. "You said you don't have addresses on your friends, but I'm sure you remember their last names."

"Hmm. I don't know." Jace squinted first one eye, then the other, appearing to search through his memory banks. "I think the long-term memory's gone. I might do better sticking to the friends I have now."

"And how many of those do you have?" When he tried to pull the deep-in-thought face again, she said, "Besides me."

A long minute passed while Jace said nothing at all and Eden finally prompted, "Well?"

He grinned that cocky devil's grin. "I'm still trying to decide if what we are is friends."

"Either we're two friends out for dinner or this is a date. Take your pick."

"You're right. Two friends out for dinner, then. It can't be a date."

"Why not?" she pressed, afraid to examine too closely the reasons for her insistence.

He lifted one shoulder in a simple shrug. "Because I've always made it a policy not to date friends."

Eden found herself recklessly pressing again. "Who *have* you dated?"

Jace laughed then, a full-throated, belly-deep laugh. "I think the better question would be, *when* have I dated. Maybe even, *if* I have dated."

"C'mon, Jace. You haven't come this far in life without a serious relationship."

"Wanna bet?" He held out a hand to shake on the deal, then reached for his glass of tea. "Don't forget who you're talking to here. Mr. Success Is Everything."

"You've never walked down the aisle?"

He finished his drink, then shook his head. "No."

"You've never been engaged?"

"No."

Sure that she shouldn't, Eden grew ever bolder. "You've never lived with a woman?"

Jace leaned forward and braced his forearms on the table. "Woman? No. Female? Well, there *is* Chelsea."

She met his lighthearted answer with a lighthearted question. "Have you ever gone steady?"

"That would be junior high, high school, right? I

can't remember." He poked his index finger at his temple. "That long-term-memory-loss thing."

One more and then she'd let him go. "Did you ever steal a kiss from a girl on the playground?"

"A-ha. Maybe there are a few cells left in the memory bank because I do remember one. But it was the soccer field, not a playground. And I wasn't the one doing the stealing."

"Do tell."

"Well, I was cut from the soccer team—"

"You told me about that. That your buddies protested with a group walk-out."

"All for one and one for all." He raised an imaginary sword. "And there was this cheerleader. She made her objections known with a bit of a mouth-to-mouth. In public."

Eden bit back a grin, tried for a stern look and failed miserably. Jace was just too much. "I see. So, you're a closet exhibitionist."

"She was the exhibitionist. I was just the . . . exhibition."

"And that's it?"

"As far as kisses go, you mean?"

"Yeah." But then the devil made her do it and she asked, "What's the best kiss you've ever had?"

"The cheerleader wasn't bad. But," he added, his eyes teasing, "I'm still waiting for the best."

"Ouch. If I were the sensitive type, I might be insulted," she said, hoping she sounded more flippant than she felt. "But since I'm not, I'm not."

"You shouldn't be. Because I haven't really kissed you yet." His gaze never wavered as he signaled the waitress and, in a move as stupid as any in her life, Eden lost her heart.

The check in his hand, Jace stood and guided her through the dining room with his warm broad palm in the small of her back. Once out the door, she shivered, her blouse no match for the cool March night or the feeling of impending change which shuddered through her.

Jace stuffed his wallet into his back pocket. "Cold?"

She shivered again, a tremor that turned to a shake. The intensity of his gaze warmed her surface doubts, but skated right over her bone-deep chill. "I'm fine."

"You may be fine, but you're shivering like it's twenty degrees. Let's get you home." With one arm draped over her shoulder, he led her to the truck.

Jace maneuvered the rolling hills like a dream and the path of Eden's thoughts dipped and climbed with the ride. The connection she felt with Jace she'd never felt with Nate. And what did that say about their relationship?

She and Nate had talked, surely. Had slept in the same bed, certainly. But they'd never flirted and teased the way she and Jace flirted and teased. They'd never played silly games of truth or dare.

Nate had never worked to understand the matters of her heart and she'd never taken the time or the care to examine his needs. That startling revelation—that in a month she knew more of where Jace had come from than she'd ever learned of Nate—unnerved her and made her wonder how long she and Jace would be able to remain just friends.

The cab grew smaller the farther they drove and, by the time they reached her place, she felt Jace on her skin. And deeper. Beneath the surface awareness to a longing sharp and sweet. A yearning beyond friendship that tingled and spread and plucked at her skin like fingers making music.

And Eden knew nothing but wanting Jace.

He pulled to a stop and reached for the key.

"Leave it running," she said, desperate to escape her confusion.

"Okay," he answered slowly, as if bewildered, then withdrew his hand and reached for the door.

"No. Don't get out."

"C'mon, Eden. I'm just gonna walk you to the door."

"I'm fine. Thanks for tonight."

He cocked back in his seat, leaning halfway against the door, one arm draped over the steering wheel, one on the back of the seat. "You gonna tell me what's wrong? You haven't spoken two words the entire trip home."

She thought about his empty barn and his guard dog, who had no one to guard him from. "Why me, Jace?"

"Why you what?"

"Out of all the people who must have crossed your path in the last three years, why did you pick me? Why did you tell me the story of your friends and your success?"

"I didn't pick you to do anything, Eden. You assigned yourself the job." He reached out and twisted a strand of her hair through his fingers. "And I have to say I'm glad. It's nice having a friend."

She looked at him, his face a light blur in the cab's dark interior. The sheen of moisture in her eyes smeared everything out of focus. It made what she was about to say easier, when she couldn't see the expression on his face.

"I know we agreed to keep this casual, but I don't want a friend right now. I want someone to hold me." She blinked, clearing her vision, her voice a frantic croak. "I want you to hold me, Jace. Only you."

Willing, for Jace, to risk everything, she lifted an unsteady hand. His gaze followed her tentative movements, the longing in his eyes a hunger as naked as a newborn babe.

She touched him the way she'd wanted to that first time, that first time so full of sensation, so new, so exciting. A rush of exploration. A testing of new waters. A rebirth of buried passions.

This time was different. This time she knew him. And she wanted to know more.

She laid her palm on his jaw, the hard structure of bone and the stubble of whiskers defining their differences, naming him man, that sweet counterpart fulfilling her needs as woman.

She stroked his brow and touched his lashes, the feathery fringe a downy soft tickle to her thumb. She slipped her fingers into his hair, the silken strands long over her wrist.

And then she leaned forward, putting herself on the line, risking a very raw part of her heart on something she wanted more than her next breath. She tendered her thumb across his lower lip, the pillow softness an elegant contrast to the rest of his purely male face.

Then she closed her eyes, curled both fists against his chest and touched her lips to his. She remembered him well. Green wood and sunshine and the simplicity of man.

He leaned back, taking her with him, cursing the gearshift under his breath. Her head found a pillow on the muscle of his shoulder and she nestled her body into his heat.

He went absolutely still, motionless, then inhaled sharply when she cuddled even closer. He expelled a long, whistling breath and she looked up. Dark need and rich urgency shone in his eyes. A ragged moan rolled from his belly.

She felt it in her hands, beneath the buttons her fingers slipped free from their holes. The rumble mellowed to a silent sigh, a breath of yearning she tasted on her tongue and held in her palms with his effort to breathe.

The hair swirling low on his belly tickled the pads of her fingers, and the tip of his tongue played a wicked game of chase with hers. His breath was hot and so was his skin, but neither came close to the heat of desire that swept through her, urging her close.

Her left hand lay trapped between Bethany and reason. So, using her right, she freed one last button, took one deep breath and searched for security in Jace's warmth. Her hand roamed with a mind of its own and she didn't dare stop. Not when his naked skin was pure heaven to touch.

Hunger spread, a wildfire arcing from his flesh to hers, or her flesh to his. The origin of the flame was not important, only the quenching of her need. She cried out when he pulled away, shuddered when he jerked the steering wheel up and whimpered when he pushed her back in her seat.

And then he joined her. Like they weren't confined in so many cubic feet of space, he scrambled over the console and, struggling with the laws of gravity and physics, lifted her onto his lap.

Her skirt rode high, the back of her thighs bare against the nubby weave of his trousers. Then he took her mouth. Her hands found a home beneath the buttons of his shirt and discovery began.

She sat in his arms, her legs draped over his, her feet propped in his seat, her fingers splayed over sleek-muscled ribs, her hip pressed against that part of him straining for deliverance. He jerked his shirt-tail free and moved her right hand to the catch of his pants.

"Touch me," he groaned, his voice thready and raw.

He smelled of desire; he tasted like man. Too impatient to deal with his clothing, Eden skimmed over the clasp and cupped him with her palm. His erection grew beneath her touch, swelling to fill her hand.

He jerked his mouth from her sore and bruised lips and rubbed his rough cheek over hers. He shuddered, pressed her face into his neck, breathed damply and rapidly against the shell of her ear.

Her struggle for breath matched his. Tiny cries caught in her throat and she twisted closer, fighting the belly that stood in the way.

His pulse thundered through the breast she'd pressed to his chest and beneath her hand, which barely contained his rising desire.

And then his hand was on her knee, feathering lightly over her skin, brushing higher and higher still. His palm spanned her thigh; his thumb brushed the cotton panties covering the swelling of her belly.

He shifted in the seat, leaning her back against the door, until his fingers found the elastic. In an instinctive move older than time, she spread her legs.

His hand breached the leg hole and she freed the clasp on his pants. His knuckles skimmed her sensitive flesh, as his zipper gave way to her demands. His fingers pressed against her, seeking entry.

She circled him with her hand, squeezing hard. He found her desire and tested her dampness. She stroked his length in response. He took her to the edge with the play of his fingers and she spread his wetness with the pad of her thumb.

"God, Eden. What are we doing?" A splintering tension held his body rigid.

"I don't know," she sobbed. "But don't you dare stop."

She panted against his throat. His answering chuckle gave way to a groan. When she squeezed again, he responded in kind, pushing her forward into a furious burst of freedom. She cried out. She gasped. She shuddered against him and he caught his release with the tail of his shirt.

Spinning slowly, Eden drifted back to earth, to reality, to the sensibility that she'd prided herself on maintaining above all else, to the sanity she'd just lost, faced with this unexpected ride into sensation. She hadn't counted on Jace, on this blast of wild seduction.

On falling in love.

A tremor shook her as Jace withdrew his hand. He reached for his fly, but she pushed him away. With more dignity than she knew she could manage, he allowed her to zip his pants.

Then he straightened her skirt, pulled her tighter in his lap and held her close, until their heartbeats mingled, until their breath misted together, until she wasn't at all sure the shudders rocking through her weren't his.

Oh, God, what had she done? Where did they go from here?

Jace exhaled raggedly. "Definitely not one of my finer moments."

"Why do you say that?" she asked, the uncertainty of the moment a sharp pain.

"I graduated from getting it on in a car way before I got out of school. I can't remember the last time I did this. I can't even remember if I ever did this." He scrubbed one hand down his face. "I'm getting old."

"You're not old."

"Then what excuse do I have for losing my mind?" he ground out.

Chagrin set in. She was as much a part of this as he was. "Don't blame yourself, Jace. I—"

"Don't blame myself? I know better." He stiffened beneath her. "I *know* better."

She sat straight on his lap, adjusted her collar, smoothed down her sleeves, stared at the fogged windshield. He caught her chin and pulled her around, and she bit her lip.

"How pregnant are you, Eden?"

"Twenty weeks."

"No. In layman's terms."

"I've got four months left."

"And what does your doctor say about sex?"

Sex. Not making love. "As long as I feel no discomfort, it's fine." She twisted her hands in her lap.

"My doctor doesn't know I'm alone. She thinks I have a disinterested partner, which at the time I began seeing her was true. But the way I figure, discomfort is the least of my problems."

"Name another."

"Logistically, sex isn't even a question. Look at this boulder I've got in the way."

"I think we worked around it just fine." He reached up to tuck a strand of hair behind her ear, stayed to cup her jaw and stroke her cheek with a tender caress.

"So what now? Do we go inside and do this right?"

She nodded, then said, "No," and felt him deflate beneath her.

"Then you'd better go in. I'm about to run out of gas."

"It has been a long day."

"Not me. The truck."

"Oh, right." The truck had been running the entire time, the whole—what, fifteen minutes, the heater keeping her warm now that she'd lost Jace's fire.

He opened the door, pivoted in his seat and set her gently on the ground. He followed her out of the truck and stripped to the waist, wadded his soiled shirt in a ball and tossed it in the floorboard of the truck.

Slamming the door, he took her elbow and guided her around to the driver's side.

He stood before her, bare-chested and brilliant beneath nature's pale moon. She glanced at her house, frowned at the light she'd left burning in the kitchen, then dropped her gaze to the ground.

"So where do we go from here?" she asked.

"Tonight we don't go anywhere. I've been as noble as I'm going to get." He kicked the rim of one tire, then stepped up close to her side.

"When you decide what you want, you know where to find me. But if you come to me, Eden, you damn well better be sure that you'll be satisfied with the little bit I can give you."

She left him standing there, her brave, injured warrior, and didn't look back until her screen door whacked behind her. Even then she allowed herself only the briefest glance.

Head hung low, he stared at the ground, shaking

his head. Then he spun around and slammed his palm flat on the bed of the truck.

The metallic cry rang again and again. And Eden's heart broke as she truly fell in love for the first time in her life.

Eden hadn't left the kitchen light burning after all. Chloe had been by. She'd dropped off her finished composite of sketches, along with the cryptic note, "At last, it is finished."

Eden thought of the frown Chloe had worn the past week and the girl's refusal to say more than she couldn't get her last piece quite right. Directing her gaze to the first picture, Eden saw nothing.

Her entire focus lay fixed on the sound of Jace gunning his engine, the screaming battle of wheels fighting gravel, the crack of the truck bottoming out against the steep pitch of her drive, the squeal of tires pressed into abuse as he laid rubber the length of Main.

Eden laced her hands until her fingers lost circulation. Drawing in one slow, deep breath, she struggled for balance in a world tilted askew. Searching for a reason to keep from running out the door and after Jace, she studied Chloe's pictures.

As she concentrated on the picture of Molly and Tucker Hansen, despair subsided, her breathing leveled, her heartbeat slowed. And Eden couldn't help but smile.

They resembled newlyweds, feeding one another a bite of Molly's brownies. Chloe was a genius, not only in her vision of inanimate objects, but in her insight to emotion,

Strangers would see Norman Rockwell America, grandparents who'd started as lovers and lived a lifetime of vows. But Eden saw more, every tiny nuance Chloe had captured.

Eden sniffed back a wealth of emotion and studied the next drawing. Chloe had added a touch of color to the face of Obadiah Parsons.

The ruddy stain highlighting his cheeks told of his struggle for perfection. One great paw of a hand cupped a pillar of wax; the other wielded a knife like an extension of his arm.

Few people saw beneath the beauty of his work or the gruff exterior of the artist. And Chloe had showed the world exactly what it was missing. A man whose artistic temperament had cost him a marriage. A man who cared for nothing now but his work.

Stone Healen's portrait told an entirely different story. At least six foot four, the gentle giant of a man wore his standard uniform of baggy overalls and long-sleeved thermal undershirt.

Not only did the top protect him from the bits of fragile glass with which he worked, it showed off a body as rock hard as his name.

He held a piece of stained glass to the light, a rainbow of cathedral colors anointing his skin. Michelangelo's *David* larger than life. A vision of male perfection waiting to explode beneath a shaft of sharp red light.

Chloe had captured the mad glint in his eye, a

man with no qualms about physically ensuring the turtle pace of his life.

Eden forced a deep breath past the wedge in her chest and moved to the picture of Nick Angelino. With an economy of strokes, Chloe had given her father life.

Hunched over his potter's wheel, sweat dripping from his brow, Nick fought to give spirit to a cold lump of clay.

Eden knew without a doubt the formless face was Chloe's mother, and that Nick was searching for the reason his wife had chosen death over him.

Chloe spared no heartache in the raw scene, but silently begged for help in the only way she knew how.

The picture at the center of Chloe's frame lifted Eden's spirits. No two people could be more at odds than John and Annette Philips. John commanded attention in bold slashing strokes, while Annette floated over the page in swirls and curves.

Eden assumed the next portrait to be of Chloe's art teacher, Jenna Priestly. Though she'd never met the petite young woman, Eden immediately sensed the bond between artist and teacher. Jenna had the patient strength a child like Chloe needed, and Eden prayed Jenna would always be there for Chloe.

The next three pictures were women Eden only knew in passing. The first was Onellia May, whom the town had quietly labeled a healer of sorts, infusing her baskets of potpourri with aromatic spells. The next portrait showed Miss Barbara, proprietress of Dolly's Clinic, tending to a one-eyed doll. Her sister, Miss Nancy, of The Coffee Bean next door, provided full-service tea parties to the owners of the recovered patients.

But it was the final picture in the row that brought Eden to her knees. Her legs buckled, along with her resolve to be strong, the minute she saw herself through Chloe's eyes.

No more than a smudged outline, she seemed to have no form at all, as if her size and shape held no importance, as if nothing mattered but her soul. And her eyes. Sharp and clean and detailed to the last lash, her eyes exuded a sparkling strength of spirit. The buoyant joy of a mother-to-be. The frightfully honest vulnerability of a woman in love with a man.

And her too-bright gaze was focused across the page at Jace.

Chloe had depicted Jace half-naked and wild, the way he'd appeared that day they'd gone to see him about the frame. His chest gleamed in the afternoon sun. The bandanna around his head resembled a pagan headdress, the carpenter's apron hung at his waist a warrior's loincloth, his stance a belligerent show of defiance.

His pale blue eyes glittered with hunger, yes, the same hunger he'd shown in the truck but more, so much more. Eden ran one finger over the black-and-white sketch, but everything she saw was in color. His deeper hunger was tempered by fear and held on a tight rein.

A small moan escaped her lips and Eden backed up. Her knees connected with a chair and, blindsided, she sat down. Why had it taken her so long to see? It wasn't regret over failing his friends that had driven Jace Morgan here. It was deeper. Something they'd both skirted the edges of more than once.

No. What Jace Morgan feared was opening himself up to be sucked into the world that had destroyed him. A world in which she kept one foot. A world he'd never be able to share with her, even should he want to share her life. They had no future. They lived their lives as depicted on the canvas—separate and apart.

Yet Jace had opened himself to her in a manner that went deeper than the physical. It meant in some way that she'd given him hope. Enough hope that he'd been willing to take the next huge step, the ultimate risk of the act of love. Jace didn't have affairs. She wondered how long he'd been celibate.

And then she wondered why she'd let desire destroy a friendship they both desperately needed. For how could they go back to that now? Now that he knew how easily she came apart at his touch. Now that she knew that she loved him.

Now that she knew what she'd once thought was loneliness was nothing compared to losing a chance she'd never really had.

NINE

"Yo, Morgan. Hand up that Phillips head, will ya?"

Jace leaned against the corner brace supporting the four-by-eight beam he stood on. He snagged the screwdriver from the belt around his waist and handed the tool to Stone Healen.

With a wave, Stone disappeared to the far side of The Emporium's roof, making less noise than Jace would've expected from a man half the other's size.

Shaking his head, he leaned down, twisted another hook into the beam and hung the length of electrical cord draped over his shoulder in place.

Why he'd ever let Molly talk him into helping out on this Festival committee thing, he still couldn't figure. But she had, and he had, and here he was, working as part of a team instead of on his own.

Long-term memory aside, he couldn't remember the last time that had happened.

Strangely enough, he liked the feeling. And though it pained him to admit it, he'd missed that good ol' boy companionship these last three years.

Even more so, he missed his friends. It was time to do something about that.

He'd told Eden he didn't have an address for Robert or Mary and he wasn't sure where in Colorado to find Kevin. But as she'd reminded him, he did have a telephone. And he knew how to dial information.

In fact, he could go one better and search any of the available Internet directories.

He was going to do that. Very soon. Set at least one part of his life to rights. Sure, he'd failed his friends, but he'd failed himself in equal measure by thinking for so long that he didn't need to make amends. Or that he could go the rest of his life on his own.

He figured Eden had a lot to do with the way he was looking at things these days, especially since, for the past eighty-four hours, she'd played a part in every thought that crossed his mind.

Today was Saturday. He hadn't seen her since Tuesday night, even though he'd spent a portion of the three days between at her place, finishing up her kitchen.

He'd managed to be there when she wasn't, or at least when she was upstairs resting. Once he heard Molly heading out, he packed up his gear and left. He just wasn't up to facing Eden yet.

And he wouldn't be until he figured out what the hell he wanted to say.

Yesterday he'd passed Chloe on his way out of The Fig Leaf. She'd walked past him without a word. Just carried her paints and brushes up the stairs like he didn't exist. No telling what kind of bad psychic vibrations were bouncing off his aura and into her uncanny mind.

No doubt she sensed he was to blame for . . . well, anything, everything, whatever. It was all about Eden.

Thinking about what had happened in his truck on Tuesday night had him hard. Eden had lit his fuse and he'd burned beneath her hands, flamed at the touch of her mouth, her fingers destroying a control he'd never before questioned. A control he'd never regain.

Even now his skin sizzled, his breathing quickened. On unsteady legs, he straightened. Shimmying his way down toward the makeshift stage area, he glanced up from securing another hook and found two of Obie Parsons's urchins watching him, bug-eyed.

It was the same awed look he'd worn when he'd watched from behind a chain-link fence as cranes hoisted steel beams into place and fearless ironworkers walked the sky overhead.

Those days had been the beginning of a dream, the tiny seed of his future. A seed that had taken root and blossomed into a forest of opportunity.

Jace looped another length of cord and damned himself for losing the focus of the goal, for allowing success to come to mean status instead of satisfaction.

And friendly rivalry to destroy friendship.

Eden had hammered and pried and dug at his deepest secrets until he was admitting things to her that he hadn't yet admitted to himself. She knew him better than anyone. Only Chelsea had seen him as naked.

And he'd sure let himself get to some sorry state when no one knew him better than his dog.

Eden had taken him apart that night in the truck, and he'd driven away physically exhausted, like they'd spent hours rather than minutes making love. Because what they'd done wasn't physical at all. The act was raw emotion, a kindred hunger.

So where do we go from here? she'd asked that night, and all he could think of was twining his fingers through hers, leading her up the stairs and following her down into blankets and bliss.

Instead, he'd gone back to his barn, to his solitary, safe way of life. Keeping his distance seemed to be the best way to keep from failing those closest to him.

If he hadn't already done that with Eden.

"John surveyed the residents this morning before the shops closed up for the dance. Profits look good." Annette Philips leaned across Eden to give Molly the word.

"I'll tell you one thing," Molly said, inclining her head in return. "No one who looked at that Angelino girl's drawings left the booth before he'd emptied his pockets. I had no idea she was so talented."

The conversation continued and Eden listened absently while all around her the evening's festivities got underway. She nibbled on a piece of grilled

chicken, not the least bit hungry, but after Molly
had gone to the trouble of fixing her a plate she
wasn't about to refuse to eat.

The lawn chair Molly had provided was comfortable enough. It just wasn't as serviceable as one of
the picnic tables scattered around the periphery of
The Emporium's parking lot.

To reach the tumbler of iced tea she'd set on the
ground, she had to lean to the right—a movement
that pitched her center of gravity offsides and threatened to capsize her chair.

Since she had no lap on which to balance her
plate, Molly had insisted on cutting Eden's chicken,
like she was three rather than thirty.

Then, to add insult to injury, she had to use the
plateau of her belly as a table—the very belly that
prevented her from sitting at the picnic tables to
begin with.

She was tired of not having a lap. She was tired
of sitting on the sidelines missing all the fun. She
was tired of being pregnant.

She felt like an invalid, an old woman, a helpless
victim of hormones. Like if she didn't have these
babies soon, she was going to come totally unglued.

Who said pregnancy had to take nine months?
Why not seven? Or even five? Why couldn't she just
sit on an egg for a couple of weeks? How did elephants stand it for a year? And how—

"Are you not feelin' well, girl?"

Eden glanced up from her destructive musings to
find Molly's never-ending compassion aimed her
way. She drew up a heartfelt smile. "I'm fine. Just

trying to figure out how I'm going to fit all the things I need to do into the little time I have left."

"Things like what?"

Eden sighed. Where to begin? "I have to take inventory now, before the twins are born—"

"Why don't I come by Monday morning?" Molly interrupted. "I'll give you a hand and—"

"I wish it were that easy," Eden cut in. "This week has been great for sales, but the store is a mess. I can't inventory until I've reorganized, which is what I should be doing now."

Instead of watching other people have fun. Instead of feeling sorry for myself. Instead of wondering about Jace.

Molly leaned forward as if to block any exit Eden might attempt. "What you should be doing now is exactly nothing." She patted Eden's knee, her touch as firm as her tone. "I told you before, if you don't take care of yourself, you won't be of any use to those babies. Business will wait."

Eden mashed the tines of her fork into her potato salad. "It's not just business. I haven't had time to buy a single thing for the twins. I don't even have diapers or sleepers or blankets or sheets. And I still have cribs to assemble—"

"Quit putting so much pressure on yourself to do everything. Take one thing at a time and take help when it's offered. Tucker or David and David Jr. can take care of those cribs tomorrow. And as for those necessities . . ."

Molly's voice trailed off and Eden glanced up in time to see her send Annette a look brimming with conspiracy. "The ladies of Arbor Glen would be pleased to give you a baby shower next Sunday afternoon."

Eden glanced from Annette to Molly and back. Her chest swelled. True friendship had never seemed so dear. So real. Or so needed. God, she missed Jace. "A baby shower?"

Annette nodded. "We've invited every female, from nine to ninety. The upstairs room in The Emporium will be perfect." She leaned back in her chair and tapped her chin with one index finger. "The only problem is color scheme. None of us know what you've planned for your nursery."

Eden pictured the mélange of color splashed over the nursery wall. Color scheme? Did Chloe even know the meaning of the term? "I never really planned anything. It just sort of . . . evolved."

"Evolved?" Annette asked. "How so?"

Eden laughed. "It's hard to explain. Why don't both of you come by in the morning and see the room for yourselves."

Molly joined Annette in setting a time, then the two women went on to share stories of previous tiny and not-so-tiny additions to the population of Arbor Glen. Eden sat back and listened with one ear.

The Emporium's parking lot faced nothing but the wide open spaces at the edge of town. She watched the last streaks of pink-gold sunlight disappear behind towers of pecans, cedars and live oaks and searched for a sense of inner calm in nature's unrelenting peace.

It wasn't any use. Her emotions ran high, gearing

up to fight the battle that had raged in her mind since Jace had driven away on Tuesday night.

Did she or did she not want Jace Morgan?

That question was too easy to answer.

She wanted him more than she wanted to breathe.

The harder question was why?

Jace made her happy. Because of him, she smiled. Because of Jace, she lost track of time. He filled her days with wild dreams, her nights with fantasies and a longing beyond bed and into the future. It was crazy, mindless, the way he consumed her every thought. And why did he?

Because of the way he made her feel?

Or because of the way she loved him?

She wanted to be his candle, to light the darkness in his soul, to burn in the window and beckon him home. She wanted to be his rain, a sweet storm of the senses. She wanted to be his warmth, a solace to his soul.

She wanted him more than anything but her children.

Darkness settled and, one by one, the hanging lanterns along the beams flicked on, bathing the sawdusted parking lot with a spectrum of muted reds and greens, yellows and blues.

Eden breathed deep; mesquite smoke and wood shavings and barbecue sauce were familiar scents, swirling with the chaos in her mind.

"So primary colors would be a safe choice?" Annette asked, clearly not for the first time.

Eden fumbled for the thread of the conversation. "As safe as anything." She pushed and pried her bulk from the chair, stretching her back when she stood. "Chloe painted a mural on the nursery wall. I don't think she missed using a color on the wheel."

Annette latched on to Eden's comment with the quick response of a reporter given a juicy lead. "You know Chloe well?"

Knowing where Annette's question was leading, Eden chose her response carefully. "I haven't known her as long as you have, but we've spent a lot of time together. She seemed to need a mother figure who didn't know much about her own mother's past. I guess I filled the bill."

Molly picked up Eden's plate and stacked it with her own. "Then Chloe must know you equally well."

Well enough to put pencil to paper and show my love for Jace.

"I guess that's a question only Chloe can answer. If you'll excuse me, I've got to run inside." She turned a pleading glance to Annette. "You don't mind, do you?"

"Not at all. Inside the back door, second door on the right."

"Thanks. And I can't wait for the shower. You're sweet to think of me," she said to Annette, then gave Molly a hug. "And thank you for being here. You're not a bad surrogate mother yourself."

"You're not leaving yet, are you?"

Eden opened wide eyes. "And miss seeing you and Tucker two-step? Not a chance."

With a quick wave, Eden headed for The Emporium. This trip to the bathroom might have saved her from the immediate threat of facing Molly and Annette's questions. But she still had to walk past the curious crowds milling around serving tables laden with smoked brisket, red beans, potato salad and jalapeño peppers.

And past the art exhibit, where speculation hung thick in the air and gossip drifted on the breeze behind the smell of red onions and Carolyn Hendricks's barbecue sauce and bread and butter pickles.

Murmurs and whispers followed Eden inside The Emporium. And even the act of latching the door behind her didn't ease her emotional vulnerability.

She knew Jace had worked this afternoon, helping set up the lighting for the dance floor. She wondered if he'd seen Chloe's picture. If he had, she hoped he hadn't returned tonight for the dance.

Facing him after Tuesday night was going to be hard enough as it was. He'd loved her completely, taken her body on a physical quest, a search for what only he could give, perfection, reverence, an explosion of sensation so great she could offer no less in return.

And she'd never be the same.

Those moments of magic were private, a secret the two of them shared. But Chloe's display was public and about as subtle as a billboard.

And Jace, being the master of privacy that he was, was not going to be happy about the whole town knowing how much she loved him, when she hadn't told him first.

* * *

Jace wished he'd never come. To this dance. To
Arbor Glen. At least when he'd arrived in town, he
should've had sense enough to stay away from Molly
Hansen. Molly got him involved in things, and the
reason he'd moved here in the first place was to stay
uninvolved.

Because of Molly, he'd met Eden. Because of
Eden, he'd met Chloe. And because of Chloe, the
entire town of Arbor Glen knew more about his feelings than any single person had a right to know—
that single person being Eden Karr.

He'd had to alter his opinion of Chloe after seeing
her sketches. She wasn't just weird. She was psychic.

No way did he walk around with that lovestruck
look on his face, the one she'd so pathetically captured. She had to have seen deeper, beneath his
skin, straight into his lumpy gray matter and
through the thick walls that hid the truths even he
didn't know.

Jace straightened, took a step back and leaned
against the trunk of an ancient spreading oak. Arms
crossed over his chest, he turned his attention to
the band, their warm-up riffs blending into his musings.

"So what are you gonna do about it, man?" Stone
Healen's voice rolled through the air in a pitch as
deep as the descending night.

Shoulders hunched, Jace stuffed his hands in the
front pockets of his jeans and propped one moccasin sole down on the base of the tree trunk. "About
what?"

Stone settled his larger-than-life body on a nearby

picnic table and propped his boots on the bench. Leaning his elbows on his wide-spread knees, he rolled a toothpick from one side of his mouth to the other, then flicked it into a mound of sawdust and bent to retie his laces.

Jace wanted to prod the other man into action, but knew Stone's stoicism rivaled the strength of his name. The man couldn't be rushed. So Jace waited.

"I don't know much about you, Morgan. I've seen you around over the years. We've said a couple of hellos. You pitched in today like someone who has a stake in this town. I appreciate hard work in a man. And I can respect your privacy. What you do is my business only if you make it so. So you tell me if I'm outta line."

Still Jace waited, finding Healen's deliberateness a trait he would've admired under any other circumstances. Right now he wanted the man to get to the point so he could get it over with.

"Go on," he nudged.

"I'm figuring by now you've seen the school art exhibit."

"Yeah; so?"

"That Angelino girl's a remarkable kid. You do the frame for her pictures?"

Jace nodded. "She told me you fixed the glass."

"That I did, but I figure she knew I'd do it before she even asked."

"Why's that?"

"After looking at the picture she drew, I think she knows me better than I know myself. It's an eerie feeling, you know."

God, but did he know.

"She did enough of whatever it is she does to make me think twice about the looks I give people. I don't think I like being as transparent as the glass I work with."

"Believe me, no one sees the things Chloe sees."

"She's got like a sixth sense then, I guess."

Sixth, seventh, eighth. Whatever it was, Jace didn't like it. "Whatever she's got, I don't want anything more to do with it."

Stone laughed, a belly-deep rumble that rolled out into the night. "Can't say I blame you, Morgan. She couldn't have painted it any plainer."

He levered himself away from the picnic table, dusted the seat of his overalls and turned his attention to the dance floor.

The band had moved from warm-ups to a full-swing "Orange Blossom Special." Sawdust flew from beneath scuffling feet as dancers two-stepped their way around the parking lot. The hanging lanterns sprinkled circles of colored light on the couples twirling beneath them, and laughter filled the air.

Jace pressed back into the tree, the isolation of the shadowed night comfortable, safe and easier to face than the questioning looks sure to come his way if he stayed.

"So what are you going to do about it?"

"I don't know." The answer was the best Jace could find, when in reality all he could hear was Eden's voice talking about the importance of friends.

She was right. He'd missed having friends.

"Eden's starting a brand-new life," Jace tentatively offered. "I'd only screw it up."

"Why don't you let the lady decide that for herself? She might just feel differently, ya know?"

Jace thought of the way she'd loved him in the truck, with no promises for the future, or thoughts beyond the moment. "I have a feeling she's already regretting some of the decisions she's made lately."

"You know her well enough to make that judgment?"

"Yeah. I do."

"Then you know better than me. But if I had a woman looking at me with that kind of love, I wouldn't hesitate to carpe diem."

Stone grew serious, from the stiffening of his stance to his somber tone of voice. "Seize the day, Morgan. It's all you've got."

In the spring evening's surprising warmth, cold took Jace, tightening his joints and pricking his skin like needles of ice. He couldn't move. He could barely find his voice.

"I thought we were talking about the way I was looking at her."

Stone turned sharply, his sandy hair falling over his forehead with the sudden movement, his eyes a study in puzzlement.

Jace drew a deep breath. Something here was out of kilter. The man never moved that fast.

A slow grin tipped the corner of Stone's mouth. The smile grew, then broadened, and a smug delight crept into his eyes—as if he had a secret and was going to enjoy the hell out of making Jace squirm before he let him in on it.

"Did you even look at the picture, Morgan?"

Jace gave a guarded nod.

"And you're saying all you saw was your own ugly mug?" Hanging his head, Stone chuckled under his breath. "Well, my man, if love ain't blind, after all."

Stone slapped Jace on the shoulder, jarring his bones and setting in motion the need to run, to escape, to write off this night as a moment in time that never happened. But he couldn't leave any more than he could make himself look at Chloe's picture again.

Having his likeness on display was bad enough. There was nothing he could do about it now. He might have a private talk with Chloe later, but the damage was done. He wasn't going to make it worse by offering his flesh and bones for further inspection.

Besides, he didn't want to chance running into Eden. Not tonight. Not this way, with the entire town salivating at her expense. So he stayed in the shadows, rooted to the ground like the century-old tree behind him.

Stone took a backward step, stopping less than two feet from Jace. "You know, Morgan, there are worse things in life than taking on another man's kids as your own." He ran a hand over his jaw and sighed. "Like not being given a chance to have kids at all."

From the cover of darkness, Jace studied Stone's face. The colored lights cast macabre patterns, torturing the man's rugged features into the semblance of a mask—half devil, half saint.

But by the time Jace blinked the visage was gone, and in its place was the handsome profile of a mountain of a man. The fit of Stone's clothes testified to incredible latent strength.

The man could crack a skull as easily as a pecan, yet used his hands to work with glass—an enigma of proportions that earned Jace's respect and at the same time stirred his curiosity.

Stone dusted his hands together. "Well, my man, I think a change of clothes is in order. I see ladies in need of a good time, and it would be insensitive of me to deprive them of that God-given right, don't you think?"

He started to leave, but then stopped and turned, slanting Jace an audacious grin. "No need to worry, Morgan. I know which lady's off limits."

Jace watched him walk away, not sure how to answer, so he didn't. With darkness complete, the focus of the night became the color-splattered square of The Emporium's parking lot, where streamers hung from the tops of the posts supporting the frame of lights.

While dancers circled the sawdusted floor, children gripped the ribbonlike strands and wove in and out, wrapping the beams like maypoles. A fey female giggle caught Jace's ear and he turned in time to see Chloe race off into the dark, a tangle of skirts behind her like the tail feathers of some exotic bird—and three teenage roosters not ten feet behind.

A wry grin stole across his face and Jace wondered if these boys had any idea what they were up against—or of the mess Chloe could make of six-teen-year-old male hormones. Then he frowned and wondered about Chloe's hormones, and decided that he was glad it was Nick's problem, not his.

He had enough hormonal problems of his own. Eden had tied him up until he felt like he'd never find the ends of the knot, or the frayed edges of what used to be a comfortable life.

He shifted his stance, the bark of the tree biting through the white oxford button-down he'd donned for the occasion. He didn't know why he'd bothered, especially since the white stood out like a beacon in the dark when all he'd come to do was see without being seen.

He'd honestly hoped to catch a glimpse of Eden tonight, but the crowd enlarged as the minutes passed until all he saw was a blur of bodies whirling to the rhythm of the songs.

This had been a stupid idea, thinking he could put things in perspective, that once he laid his eyes on Eden the memory of that night wouldn't seem so hot, her skin so soft, her mouth pure heaven, her hands sweet agony, her scent . . . apricot and spring wind and . . . close.

He knew she was there by the stirring in his blood, the sharpening of his senses, the storm of raw emotion that seethed in his soul. His hands shook, so he leaned back against them and watched her approach. Tiny steps carried her to him, and she seemed to bend beneath the burden she carried.

He damned his inability to offer more than friendship.

And then he damned his cowardice.

Five feet away she stopped and ran her index finger along the edge of the table where Healen had sat. Her smile trembled, the corners of her mouth fighting her indecision. Whatever she felt, she was no more comfortable than he. That made him feel better. He guessed.

"I didn't know if you'd be here."

Quiet and testing, her voice drifted to him through the low-hanging branches of the tree.

"Neither did I," he answered, whether referring to himself or Eden he wasn't quite sure. "Thought I'd stick around a while, though. Make sure there's no problems with the wiring."

"The place looks great. You all did a good job."

"Yeah, well, the lanterns were Molly's idea. Those and the ribbons."

Eden twisted her hands until her fingers appeared bloodless. The nervous gesture increased Jace's unease. He swallowed hard and looked up. His gaze devoured her profile; the colored lights magnified the extent of her exhaustion, the country and western guitar a background meter for her labored breathing.

What the hell was she doing here?

Staring toward the dance floor, she released a small sigh. "Once Molly sets things in motion, it takes an act of God to stop the ball from rolling."

That, or the act of a fool. "She's a pistol, all right.

Thinks the town would fall apart without her holding it together.

"She's certainly done her best to keep me in one piece. I owe her a lot for sending you my way." She glanced at him only briefly, as if eye contact was out of the question. "You did a good job, Jace. My kitchen. The shop. Everything looks great. I should've thanked you sooner."

Small talk. He hated it. "I've got some cleanup to do. I'll try to get to that tomorrow."

"Don't worry about it. I can—"

"No. You can't." He cut her off, not liking the way she'd so quickly dispatched him from her house, from her life. "It's my mess. I'll clean it up."

"Fine," she said, stiffening. "But I thought you'd be glad of the offer. You know, anything to keep you out of my house."

"Why do you say that?"

"Give me a break, Jace. After the way you've avoided me all week it's obvious that the sooner you wash your hands of me the better."

He pushed off the tree and shoved both hands through his hair. "Is that what you think I've been doing? Avoiding you?"

"Haven't you?" She finally turned to face him.

He let his hair fall, lowered his hands and settled them at his hips. "I thought I was giving you your space."

"My space?" Her eyes widened, flashing green fire. "When did I ever ask for my space?"

Sarcasm didn't usually come so thick. At least not

from Eden. Jace shored himself up and said, "You didn't. Not in so many words."

"Then how?" she demanded.

He took a step toward her. "What the hell was I supposed to think after the way you walked away Tuesday night? You made your feelings pretty damned clear."

"The way *I* walked away? Try the way you pushed me away, Jace. The way you shoved me. The way you gave me ultimatums."

She stepped closer, moving in for the kill. "What I've been doing since Tuesday night is calling myself a fool for beating my head against a brick wall."

"Is that what I am? A brick wall?"

"You're about as unyielding as one. It's your way or no way. I think that pretty much sums up what you said."

Her final step brought her close enough to touch. He didn't, but she did, making her point with the index finger she jabbed against his chest.

"You pushed me away then, like you're pushing me away now. I'm not going to let you run over me. You may feel you did that to your other friends, but I'm strong enough to make sure it's not going to happen to me. I don't play that way. And I'm not going to let you play that way either."

Silence hung between them as Jace absorbed her words. Once he did, he froze. The implications staggered him, but he wasn't about to share that little secret. Still, he needed to know.

"Then when you told me that you didn't want a friend, that you wanted me . . ."

"I meant it."

He caught her hand before she backed away and held her there, afraid to let go and find out that he was holding on to nothing but a futile hope. "And what happened in the truck . . ."

"Is what I wanted to happen," she whispered, her smile a clear sign that he wasn't as adept at hiding his feelings as he'd once been.

Or maybe what he felt for Eden was something he just couldn't hide.

"Are you blaming yourself for that night?" she asked, working her fingers free to splay both hands on his chest. "Couldn't you tell that I was right there with you? Don't you know that what I offered, I offered honestly? That what I took, I took selfishly?"

Jace shut his eyes. The inky blackness of night offered welcome relief. "Then what *we* did . . ."

"Was real, Jace. As real as it gets. No subterfuge. No lies. No ulterior motives. I wanted you." Her voice fell then, as her strength of conviction failed. "And I thought you wanted me, too."

Jace sucked a sharp breath through his teeth. The way he'd wanted her then was nothing compared to the way he wanted her now. Body and soul, under his skin, breathing his air . . . forever. He couldn't stop the moan that caught in his throat any more than he could stop himself from crushing her to him.

He didn't remember her feeling so good, or like she belonged to him. But this time he swore he'd remember everything. He stepped back into the shadows, drawing her with him, leaned against the tree trunk, pulling her close—as close as two people could get with so much still unsettled between them.

Her belly seemed so much a part of her now that he didn't think twice about the way she nestled against him. At the base of his neck, he felt her warm cheek, her warmer breath and hot, silent tears. Her whimper was an echo of the sound in his throat that he couldn't find the strength to let go.

But then she touched her lips to the curve of his jaw, tasted his skin with the tip of her tongue, and what clawed at him then was a simpler need, one that knew nothing of risk.

That only knew she was his.

TEN

A slow lover's ballad soughed through the air. "So, as long as we're here, do you wanna dance?"

It was all Jace could think of to say. Not that he wanted to dance. In fact, never moving at all suited him just fine. But sooner or later someone would notice them standing like statues entwined.

And neither one of them needed the gossip.

She snuggled tighter, her arms slipping around his waist, her hands roaming down to his hips. "As long as we don't have to move."

His feelings exactly. "I think that's the whole point, Eden. You know, dancing. *Moving* to music."

She shook her head and laughed. "No. I mean as long as we don't have to move from this spot." Her hands found their way deep inside the back pockets of his jeans and she glanced at the crowded dance floor. "I'm not up to a crush of bodies right now."

Jace wasn't about to argue. The only body he wanted crushed next to his was Eden's.

"C'mon," he said, wrapping one arm around her shoulders, reluctant to let her go even for the time it took to walk to the far side of the tree.

The few extra feet took them out of the reach of the brightest lights and into the dark shadows of the tree. The distance would also hopefully dissuade any well-meaning townsfolk from crashing their private party.

Now that he had Eden all to himself, he damn sure didn't intend to share these intimate moments.

Though Eden's shape made for a difficult slow dance, Jace had no complaints. He took her hands in his, secured them around his neck, then wrapped himself around her like warmth from the sun.

She tangled her fingers in the length of his hair and tangled her breath with his. He tasted her in the air, drew her into his mouth, the very way he'd wanted.

Her head on his shoulder, her lips on his neck, she rocked against him, an awkward swaying of bodies more precious than a first kiss. He smoothed back her hair and tenderness swelled, the unfamiliar emotion lulling his senses.

What, besides nothing, had he done to deserve her?

Jace lingered there, in the shadows, and absorbed only Eden. He closed his mind and opened his heart.

And then his body took over.

The way they stood was too close for dancing, the way they moved nonexistent. Their rhythm was fluidly smooth, their motion sleepy and slow.

When he pressed his thumb to her throat, Eden's pulse quickened. His own heart responded with a steady rise in tempo and a rapid pumping of blood.

He dropped a kiss at her hair, at her temple and her brow, then reached up to release her hold on his neck. "Eden, give me your hands."

She smiled against his neck and nuzzled even closer, rich female satisfaction in the chuckle that rose in her throat. "No. I want you right where you are."

Her comment only made his blood pump harder, his arousal thicken. But, hell, if she didn't mind, then neither did he. This was his fantasy, after all, his time to steal until one of them woke up from this madness-induced dream.

For that's what he was—crazy—for thinking anything would be different after tonight, for thinking she wouldn't wake up tomorrow, or the next tomorrow, or the one after that and start making plans to leave town, to return to a life he could never be part of.

Wasn't that reason enough to turn and walk away?

He staggered backwards and came up against the tree, spread his legs and pulled her between. She came without question, cuddling against him like he really had something to give her, like no place else would do.

His own feelings made even less sense, because he knew in her arms he'd find out exactly who he was. And that scared more than the hell out of him.

With no pretense left between them, with common sense dispatched, he lowered his head. She was waiting, like she'd expected him back, like she wanted him back, like he belonged. Her mouth

opened, her hands roamed and he could barely concentrate on one for the other.

And this time he wanted to go slow.

He kissed her thoroughly, giving no thought to
time or place, only to Eden and her mouth, the way
her lower lip trembled, the way she nipped him with
her teeth, the way she seemed to smile like she held
all the cards in this game.

But Jace could only play for so long. Especially
when her tongue stroked his, her movements slow,
seductive, a striptease of the senses. Oh, God.

And he'd thought sex in the seat of his truck was
intimate. Nothing topped what Eden was doing to
his mouth.

Heat grew, and with it longing, a building of sexy
steam. He tunneled his hands into her hair, holding
her still before he went off. Intoxicating, drugging,
her mouth refused to stop, working at his, tiny
strokes of tongue, hot breath and whispered words
of wicked want.

Slow was out of the question.

Her hands wandered to the waistband at the back
of his jeans—jeans too tight for the strain in front.
But she fought her way inside. She skimmed the tail
of his shirt, bunching material, wadding it in her
hands until her fingers found his naked buttocks.

She laughed then, a girlish giggle that knotted
him up. "Jace Morgan, where are your drawers?"

"I was in a hurry," he managed. Her fingers
inched around to his side, her thumb finding the
crease where hip met thigh, getting too close for
comfort.

So he decided it was time to get even.

He leaned back, putting enough space between their bodies to discover the shape of her very shapely breast. It filled his palm and then some, the sexy curves swollen with pregnancy and desire.

At her sudden intake of breath, he thought he'd gone too far, until she took his hand in hers and pressed harder, showing him how to touch her, to arouse her, to make her moan.

She moaned again, then yelped, and he knew this time was different, especially when she backed away wide-eyed and pressed her hands low on her abdomen.

"Eden? What—"

"A contraction."

Christ! "Now?"

"A false one. The first one I've felt." She gave a tremulous laugh. "Oooh. Bethany felt it, too. Don't worry, my sweet," she crooned, stroking the left side of her belly. "It'll be over soon."

"Eden?" His heart thudded; his voice shook.

"I'm fine."

Not even marginally relieved, Jace scraped a hand down his jaw. "Are you sure?"

She nodded, and concern creased the corners of her eyes. "I'd better get home, but I want you to understand this doesn't mean I'm leaving."

He felt like a three-year-old. "I'm a jackass, Eden. I'm not stupid."

The corner of her well-kissed mouth tipped in a grin. "There's a difference?"

He scowled, then reached out and buried his

hand in her hair, drawing her close. "Can I ask you one thing?"

"Sure," she answered, breathless.

"If we ever start this again—"

Her tongue darted out to wet her lips. Then his. *"When* we start this again, you mean."

Once he'd guaranteed his own heart failure, he pulled away from her slick mouth. Taking a deep breath, he looked her straight in the eye.

"When we start this again, can we make sure we're in a position to finish it?"

Pouting as she thought, she cocked her head to one side. "Physical position or emotional?"

"Physical, for sure. But emotional would work."

"I'll sleep on it," she answered, giving him one very tired wink.

He'd rather she slept on him, but as he'd said, he wasn't stupid. So instead, he walked her home.

Light from the sidewalk lamppost at the corner of The Fig Leaf sparkled through the etched-glass window on the shop's front door.

Eden dropped the bottle of window cleaner in the bucket at her feet, straightened the freshly washed lace curtains, then, fists in the small of her back, stretched out her own kinks as well.

She hadn't had another pain since the one that so rudely interrupted her reunion with Jace two hours earlier. Not that she didn't welcome the sharp reminder of how little time she had left—and what all she had left to do.

But she wasn't quite ready for her life to turn upside down. Not yet. She had too much to settle with
Jace before Beth and Ben arrived to consume her
attention, her energy, her every waking moment.

She needed time.

Time with Jace. Private time. Long, quiet hours.
Laughter-filled minutes. Days and weeks to sort the
risks from the challenges, the facts from the feelings,
the rights from the wrongs.

Or maybe what she really needed was guidance.

Unless she could figure a way to clean up her so-
called love life as fast as she'd cleaned up her shop.
Her shop. She loved her shop, the way with every
passing day it felt more and more like home—and
less like a stop on life's road.

Turning to survey two good hours of work, she
decided the hardwood floor still needed a good buff-
ing. But until she could get to The Emporium and
rent a buffer from John, the light coat of wood
cleaner she'd mopped on would have to do.

She'd refolded and aligned the stacks of jumpsuits
stored in the cubbyholes Jace had built, then moved
the placemats and tea towels from the old set of
shelves to the new.

With the hanging garments spaced on the racks
at one-inch intervals, she'd tackled the corner of
baby things, draping a tumbling blocks quilt over
the back of a miniature white wicker sofa.

The two antique dolls that sat there now wore her
favorite christening gowns, and the patchwork teddy
bear propped between sported a jaunty bib of his
own.

Seized by an uncontrollable urge, she'd finished the display by covering the trio with the silver and gold baby blanket she thought of as belonging to Jace.

She remembered the first day she'd seen him, the way he'd played the big bad wolf to her little lamb. She'd known even then that he was a phoney. His brusqueness had only succeeded in making her wonder who he was.

She no longer wondered who. Or why. She knew exactly what thoughts had been going through his mind. And exactly how he'd felt reliving his past, thinking of the friends he'd lost touch with, the families they'd started, the careers they'd advanced.

He'd be contacting them soon, she just knew it. And that pleased her more than she would've imagined.

She headed for the second floor to take advantage of this curious burst of energy. She set her bucket of cleaning supplies at the foot of the stairs, stopped in the kitchen for an extra roll of paper towels and decided to do something about Jace's mess when she got there.

He said he'd get to it tomorrow, but for some bizarre reason that wasn't soon enough. So while she had the drive and the time, she did what she could, tossing the scraps of molding into a paper bag along with the old hinges and screws.

She found a discarded shipping box big enough for the few tools still lying on the floor and pitched fragments of Sheetrock into the trash.

With that little bit accomplished, she dusted her hands together and wrinkled her nose. And sneezed.

Might as well wipe down the countertops.

And the sink.

And the stove.

She double-checked the cupboards, switched the shelves of tumblers and coffee mugs in one, then rearranged the jars on her lazy Susan spice rack in another. While she was at it, she cleaned the window over the sink and the smaller one set into the door.

Then she mopped.

With a sense of urgency she purposefully shoved aside, she finally headed upstairs. Her bedroom didn't take more than a minute or two; just a quick change of sheets and a fluffing of the lace throw pillows in the dormer window.

Wanting to make sure her loosest jumper was pressed for tomorrow, she opened the closet. Finding what she wanted, she decided there was really no need to keep all her old business suits on hangers.

A trip downstairs yielded a lawn-size leaf bag. She folded the remnants of her old life into neat stacks and shoved the bag into the back of the closet. Later she'd decide between charity or resale; charity or resale or storage. Funny how she had to stop and add the latter to those options.

The bathroom came next, but once she saw her reflection—the unusual brightness in her eyes, flushed cheeks and wild halo of mahogany hair—she supposed a long soak might help ease whatever it was that had her so keyed up.

Ten minutes later, up to her chin in scented bubbles, eyes closed, toes tapping the end of the tub, she knew it wasn't going to work.

Where had this energy come from? And where had it been when she'd needed it, the past three weeks? With a defeated sigh, she toweled off, then slipped into her panties and bra and a long button-front cotton jumper.

The only room left on which she could vent this cleaning fury was the nursery.

Securing her hair in a topknot, she padded barefoot down the hall. Now, before she got everything set up, would be the perfect time to do one final cleanup and make a list of everything she needed to buy.

Two steps inside the door, she forgot why she was there, filled with the wonder of what this room made her feel. The almost terrible sense of rightness, like if she gave in to her feelings and shouted her joy to the sky the bubble of gladness would burst.

Maybe that's why reaching for Jace scared her so. Loving him was such a risk. She wanted him desperately, and knew he wanted her, too.

She crossed the nursery to the windowseat, peered out at the twinkles of light in the sky. "Star light, star bright, first star I see tonight . . ."

Turning around, she raked a critical glance over the nursery. This is where her children would begin an incredible future. This nursery would be perfect, even if Beth and Ben didn't know a thing about it.

The south wall was bare, and that's where she'd place the cribs, end to end, out of any drafts from

the window and the spill of light from the hall. An
antique dry sink sat inside the door.

She'd padded the top to use as a dressing table,
and after this weekend's shower she'd stock the bottom with diapers and sleepers and gowns.

The north wall was Chloe's masterpiece, and Eden
couldn't bear to cover it. She'd already imagined
long lazy mornings propped in the cushioned windowseat feeding first Benjamin, who was sure to be
most demanding, and then Bethany, whose docile
nature would give her a rare strength of her own.

She'd huddle up with her sweet babies, snuggle
down into the mountain of multicolored pillows and
weave magic tales of the creatures on the wall.

Of the blue and yellow butterflies, who were really
tiny fairies sprinkling magic dust in the air. Of the
trio of elves that slept in every red poppy, safeguard-
ing the creatures living in the green woods beneath.
Of the enchanted winged animals, flying away to
freedom and opportunity—the same things she
would give to her babies.

She'd rock them to sleep at night, and . . . and . . .

She didn't have a rocking chair. Oh, God, she
didn't have a rocking chair. How could she not . . .
of all things . . .

Oh, God, she needed a rocking chair.

With her fingers pressed to her lips, she took a
deep breath. Her sense of calm returned, along with
a new sense of purpose. She knew the rocking chair
she wanted.

The rocking chair she needed.

Now.

* * *

Chelsea met her at the door of the barn and padded silently alongside as Eden walked through the dimly lighted woodshop. The rocker sat where she remembered and, though tempted to sink down and rock her suddenly exhausted body to sleep, Eden headed for the staircase in the far corner of the shop, still wondering what foolishness had driven her here.

Her sense of desperation had no logical basis. She knew that. Logically. But knowing she was running on high-octane emotion gave her need to put her house in order an acute edge.

She stood at the bottom of the staircase feeling stupid, almost nauseous and totally tongue-tied. What was she going to say to explain away her impromptu visit? Why hadn't she called?

It was eleven thirty P.M., for chrissakes.

At least Jace appeared to be up, judging from the bass beat booming down and the sliver of light shining from beneath his door. She screwed up her courage and moved onto the first step.

Chelsea exploded, a blinding flash of silver fur, a rapid-fire fit of barking and a low-throated feral growl. Again. And again. Eden froze and plastered herself against the wall.

A spotlight from above flooded the staircase. The door shot open. Jace stood in silhouette.

"Eden, what the hell? Chelsea. Cool it!" Jace bounded down the stairs. Chelsea dropped at Eden's feet, tail wagging, an apologetic smile on her doggy face.

An hysterical giggle bubbled from Eden's throat. "Chelsea, cool it? What kind of obedience school did you send her to, Morgan?"

Reaching her side, Jace grasped her wrist. Her pulse fluttered erratically beneath his touch. He glanced at her face.

"You okay? Is it the babies?"

She shook her head. "It's stupid. Really. I'll just go back home. Forget I was ever here."

She tried to back away, but he cupped her elbow and guided her up the stairs.

"You come out here at near midnight, your pulse beating like a wild thing, and you think I'm gonna let you go? Think again."

"I owe the pulse to your dog. Guess you're glad to know your Alaskan security system's in perfect working order."

She stepped over his threshold; he closed the door behind her. Slowly, she turned.

A towel hung around his neck. His hair trailed in wet clumps to his shoulders. He smelled of sweat. The Houston Astros T-shirt stretched across his chest was sizes too small. His gray jersey shorts hid nothing of what he was. And his bare legs were as gorgeous as the rest of him.

She swallowed hard and dropped her gaze to the floor, and the baggy white crew socks sagging at his ankles.

Jace released her and headed for the black lacquer entertainment center stretching the width of one wall. He lowered the volume on what sounded like heavy metal without the heavy and returned to her side.

"Look, Eden, I just finished working out. I'll run take a shower and we can talk."

It was then that she saw the huge work-out setup in the middle of the floor. It seemed to be his only furniture, but for the futon folded out in the corner.

"I really only came for the rocking chair."

He dragged his hands down his face in weary confusion. "The rocking chair?"

"I know. It's stupid." She gestured expansively with her hands and began to pace. "But after you took me home I started cleaning up in the shop, and in the house, and got to the nursery and realized I don't have a rocking chair."

Silence settled, a thick tension into which they did no more than breathe. Jace blinked. A bead of sweat rolled down his temple to his throat, and Eden measured his visible pulse against her own.

Finally, he blew out a weighty sigh and placed both hands on her shoulders. The imprints of his fingers warmed her back.

"Eden, you could've called if you needed the rocking chair." He backed her up until her knees hit the weight bench. "Sit here while I shower. I'll be back in ten minutes and we'll talk."

She nodded and watched him walk away. It was all she could manage amid her confusion. Once he'd gone, she glanced around, grounding herself. Jace's words shattered any self-delusion of why she was here.

The loft was one huge low-ceilinged room. In a far corner alcove, copper-bottom pots hung suspended over a butcher block. A single bar stool kept sentinel beside it. Off to the right, a shuttered folding screen shielded a second recessed area. The sound of running water flowed from behind.

She turned. A brass floor lamp cast a circle of light over the black-covered futon, leaving the rest of the room in semishadow. The pale, cream-colored walls softened the stark severity of the room.

Eden leaned back against the inclined headrest and propped her arms on the butterfly extensions. With her legs crossed at the ankle, she stretched out the length of the bench.

And that's when she noticed the pictures. Eighteen black-on-cream mattes and ebony frames boldly displayed pieces of Jace's past. Framed pencil sketches of impossible buildings, black-and-white drawings of fantasy homes, skylines without end.

His talent balanced Chloe's in a structured sort of way, but his imagination was her equal. And he'd suppressed this incredible gift, along with so much else of himself because he'd allowed his success to destroy him.

But God, he still dreamed. He denied it all, but he still dreamed. Keen-edged compassion stung Eden's eyes, constricting the band of tension pressing down on her chest.

She exhaled long and forever, knowing she'd come here seeking solace. But now she couldn't leave without giving Jace the same.

She drew up her legs as far as pregnancy allowed,

tucked her skirt under the toes of her ballet flats and leaned her forehead on her knees. The water stopped running.

She waited.

A door opened.

She waited.

The scent of soap and dampness drifted into the room.

And the waiting grew taut.

Without looking up, she knew he was there. Her heart pattered sharply in her chest. She curled her toes and ran damp palms down her shins, smoothing the cotton jumper along with her nerves.

Wearing nothing but red jersey shorts, Jace straddled the bench. Eden closed her eyes as his weight settled at her feet.

With the barest pressure of one finger, he lifted her chin. "Look at me, Eden."

Oh, God, she couldn't. Not with so much bare skin and so few clothes between them.

"Eden. Look at me." He leaned forward; his breath fanned her temple. His hair smelled like the deep woods, dark and green and earthy, a place she wanted to get lost in, to escape from the beginnings of arousal trailing through her.

She opened her eyes. Jace's sizzled, and the steamy burn heated her blood. Was she ready for this? What a question. This was exactly why she'd come.

She rubbed the toes of her shoes in a nervous gesture; her fingers brushed his inner thigh. She left them there, and he didn't move back, just lifted his leg, brushing rough hair along the tips of her nails.

She shivered and patted the side of the bench. "You work out on this thing every night?"

"Some nights longer than others."

"Tonight?"

"About the longest. Pretty much maxed myself out."

"Then I should go," she said, though she made no move to do so. "You're probably tired."

"No." He inched closer, spread his legs wider.

Desire rose in Eden's throat, then dropped to her chest where she couldn't breathe anyway.

"I'm not tired," Jace went on. "Just trying to work off some excess energy. I don't think it helped."

Not a bit, judging from the taut lines of his body.

"I know how you feel. I went home thinking how nice it would be to crash after this Spring Fest week. Instead, I spent three hours cleaning my house."

"And you're not tired either."

"No." She took a sighing breath. "I sometimes wonder if I'll ever get a full night's sleep again."

"So what's this about the rocking chair?" he asked, fingering the edge of her hem where it brushed her toes.

"It sounds so ridiculous now. But I was upstairs in the nursery picturing how it will look once everything comes together and I realized I don't have a rocking chair."

"And you needed it tonight."

She lifted one shoulder. "Just one more thing I needed to settle."

"So here you are."

He'd moved up her leg now, his fingers running the scale from her ankle to her knee.

"Yeah. Here I am."

He reached her thigh, spread his fingers wide and squeezed. "Did you come for the rocker? Or did you come to settle things with me?"

She wasn't used to demands for honesty from anyone but herself. And this type of honesty was the hardest of all, for it could change her life. "What do we have to settle?"

His gaze charred a hole through her resolve. "What *don't* we have to settle? There's so much business unfinished between us, we could be here all night. If I'm the real reason you've come."

His words scared her and rightfully so. "I'm frightened, Jace."

He made a sound then, a laugh that held no humor, or a ripping apart of his soul. She couldn't tell. He took her hands, splayed them on his chest. "You think I forgot to dry off here? No, baby, this is absolute terror."

Her hands lingered, testing the slickness of his skin, feeling his heart thunder through her fingers. "What do you have to be afraid of?"

"You. Me. Me hurting you." His finger trailed along the edge of her scooped neckline, dipping beneath, running the swells of her breasts.

He flicked open her jumper's top button with his finger, flicked the second with his thumb. "Taking chances. Not taking chances. Reaching out. Holding back. The same things that frighten you."

A third button opened, a fourth popped free. The heat welling from his skin seared her flesh. With trembling fingers, she gripped his hand, holding on while he loosened the next four buttons to her waist.

Short and shallow, her breath rushed from her lungs. "Then we're in no better position than we were three hours ago."

"The physical we can work around. The emotional, well . . . one thing at a time." Another button. Another, and he reached her knees.

Glimpses of her serviceable cotton panties and her sturdy maternity bra peeked through the widening gap. She wished for nothing more right now than to be decked out in satin and lace.

For Jace to see her this way the first time brought unexplainable tears to her eyes. "So what are you doing? Making a move or taking a chance?"

He released the final button, the one at her hem, then sat back and braced his palms on his thighs. "Both."

She choked back a sob, caught her lower lip between her teeth. Her body ached; her fat, ugly, traitorous body ached, wanting to give him pleasure, to hold him close, to take him inside and show him her love without speaking the words.

But how could she, when she couldn't even see her own damn feet?

"Are those tears, Eden? Do you want me to take you home?"

What she wanted she couldn't put into words, and a big hole in the floor right about now would save her from having to try.

"What's wrong?"

She sniffed back a wad of misery, huddled in on herself to hide her glaring imperfections. "What I want is to please you, but how can I when I'm so fat and—"

"Oh, baby." He put his hands on her shoulders and pushed her upright, making sure her gaze was trained on his. "You're not fat. You're pregnant. And you please me just by being here. If you don't want to take this any further—"

"I do," she interrupted, shocked at her own temerity. "I just don't see how—"

He stopped her words with a quick, hot kiss. "That's all I wanted to hear."

He rose then and crossed the room, easing up the music's volume until the bass beat low in the pit of her stomach, intensifying the throb nesting there.

Clutching the parted edges of her jumper in tight fists, Eden licked her lips. Anticipation coiled madly; a steady stream of sensation tightened the ball of writhing nerves burning like hot coals at her center.

Jace lowered the light, sending the room into shadows, images, dark shapes and darker fantasies. A rustle of cloth, and Jace returned.

Naked.

Eden's imagination shut down, faced with such riveting reality. Light brushed him intimately, shading and contouring with free will. His muscled chest and flat belly she'd caressed. His buttocks she'd molded with her palms. And his powerfully built legs she'd glimpsed for the first time tonight.

But the other part of him nestled so proudly between his legs took her breath away. The beauty of his living flesh rendered her tactile memory vain.

She'd touched him and stroked him and made him come, but she'd never imagined the naked picture as a whole and found herself in awe of his stunning male perfection.

"God, you're beautiful." Her whisper drifted into the darkness.

He spread his shorts on the padded bench, straddled the cloth and sat, settling himself at her feet. He removed her shoes and dropped them to the floor. His thick length rested on the top of her feet, the softness below on her toes.

"No, Eden. You're beautiful." He reached up, pulled the barrette from her hair; his hand lingered along the shell of her ear, the slope of her jaw, her neck.

His gaze never wavered, his eyes a blue flame of seduction. With sure fingers, he parted her jumper, slipped it from her arms, sending it into a heap behind her.

"So beautiful," he whispered, then leaned over and touched trembling lips to hers.

Both palms against his jaw, she caressed his face, her fingers shaking, the stubble of his beard an erotic marking of their differences.

He gripped her shoulders, deepening the kiss, claiming her mouth with a fierce sweep of his tongue. Her hands slid to his biceps to hold on. He scooted closer. She felt him pulse and lengthen and grow harder still.

Her feminine response started deep inside, seep-

ing down to ease his entry. He groaned, a tortured
sound, released her shoulders and palmed the backs
of her knees as he lifted her legs over his. The backs
of her thighs tingled, her smooth skin scraped by
his coarse hair. He moved in closer, pressing against
her, his erection full between them.

He feasted at her mouth, tiny strokes of his tongue
on her lips, longer minutes spent learning the limits
of a kiss. There were none, she discovered, only the
agony of waiting and wanting more. Slick tongue
rode slick tongue, a thrusting setup for the most
intimate act yet to come.

She gripped the back of his knees, her anchor in
his storm, and rode the swells of ebb and tide; first
avid hunger, then a sated lull before passion lured
them back to the fiercely wild, openmouthed kiss.

Hooking her feet in the small of his back, she
pulled him closer, feeling his heat through panties
grown damp.

He let go of her legs and reached back for the
clasp of her bra. Eden shrugged it off, watched his
eyes heat and flare, and responded to his gaze with
a hard clench of her thighs. Then she leaned back,
offering Jace her swollen breasts.

His eyes misted and glazed. Chest forward, head
back, she arched her neck, gripped the bars overhead for support and held on. Jace leaned forward,
trailing gentle kisses over the upper swells, the
plump undersides. Her engorged nipples peaked at
the touch of his tongue.

He suckled hard, pulling her deep into the
warmth of his mouth. A whimper crawled from her

throat and she dug her heels into his buttocks. Deep
below her womb, bones shifted and stirred, crying
for him to come home.

His hands moved to her cotton-covered belly and
stroked, moving lower, as if taking measure of how
they would fit. He lifted his head, returned his
mouth to hers and moved both hands to the waistband of her panties on her right.

"You got more of these at home?" he growled.

She only nodded. She couldn't talk with his
tongue in her mouth.

The sound of tearing fabric ripped through the
air. First one side, then the other, and her panties
no longer proved any obstacle, or barrier, or safety
net. She was vulnerable now, spread wide open with
no going back. It was a trip she was eager to travel.

He strung kisses over the mound of her belly, her
navel, the stretch marks at her sides. And Eden died
a little more with each touch of his lips, each sexy
foray of his tongue.

She was ready to explode by the time his knuckles
grazed her thighs, from one leg to the other.
Through the thatch of curls between her legs. Back
and forth. Over and over. The barest touch of a butterfly's wings, the sweet brush of promised heaven.

"God, Eden. You smell like apricots. Like long,
hot, sexy summers. Like warmth." He lifted his head
then, moved his lips to her mouth. "I've been cold
so long. Eden, baby, please make me warm."

She tilted her hips up in answer. The tip of his
erection, full and ripe, pressed against her. She
gripped the padded bars of the butterfly extensions,

and Jace settled his hands beneath her hips, pulling her forward until she sat on her spine.

The muscles of his thighs flexed beneath the back of hers and he eased inside, a slow, steady entry that went on forever. Eden prayed like she'd never prayed before. That they were doing the right thing, that regrets wouldn't destroy this new beginning.

But then Jace moved, wiping all concerns from her mind, her only conscious thought the velvet stroke of his body in hers. He loomed above her like some pagan god, his skin burnished with captured gold, a fine sheen of sweat and lamplight turned low, his wet hair a crown of jet adorning his head.

And his eyes. Oh, God, his eyes. The fiery blue demanded her worship, the sacrifice of her very soul. She offered more, planting her feet on his thighs and lifting up to meet his thrusts.

He slowed then, drew a whistling breath between clenched teeth. "Eden. Stop. Christ, please stop." The broken words rolled out on a growl. "Slow, baby, slow. I don't want to hurt you."

But she was mindless now, coming undone, splintering with sharp, urgent need. "Don't stop, Jace. Never stop."

She hooked her heels around his hips, pulled him forward again and again. His fingers gouged her backside and he held her still, sliding slow and deep, his body one coiled spring, his face a tortured mask of control.

She wanted to set him free.

She reached between their tangled limbs, finding

the source of sensation, and created a fire of her own. Her fingers barely met around the base of his slick shaft, but she squeezed, drawing a ragged groan from his gut. She dipped lower, fondled the heaviness beneath. Jace cried out, increasing the tempo, firing the friction to a fevered pitch.

"Don't . . . want . . . to hurt you."

His harsh words snagged on her fractured heart.

"Oh, man. Oh, man." His legs strained as his body moved, sending her spiraling to the edge. Closer. Closer. Until she lost her hold and surrendered to pure sensation.

Jace exploded with her, a guttural cry spilling from his throat. The force of his climax lifted them both from the bench. He buried his face in the crook of her neck.

The moisture from his hair cooled her skin.

The damp trail of his tears broke her heart.

ELEVEN

"I owe you a huge apology."

Jace held Eden curled close to his side in the crook of his arm. The tub he'd installed in his loft was worthy of a Roman bathhouse—appropriate, considering the orgy to his senses he still hadn't recovered from.

"What could you possibly have to be sorry for?" Eden shifted to one side on the middle of the three sunken steps. She leaned into him, her belly snug against his waist.

The female anatomy just amazed him. He ran his hand over the curve of her stomach, and a ripple of motion stroked his palm in return. So white, so smooth, her flesh glowed against his own darker skin. "Protection. We didn't. I didn't. I should have. I'm sorry."

Water slapped and gurgled around his chest as Eden sat full upright, dislodging his hand. He couldn't decipher the look in her eye, so he shifted uneasily beside her.

"Well, we certainly don't have to worry about me getting pregnant."

"True. But that's not all protection's about."

"When was the last time you were with a woman, Jace?"

"Hmm. Well . . . it's been a while." When her look insisted, he reluctantly added, "All right, all right. Not since before I moved here from Dallas."

A look of surprise flitted through her eyes before she shuttered her lashes down.

He frowned. "You don't believe me?"

"Of course I believe you. It's just hard to imagine, that's all."

"What, that I can't control my baser instincts?" The first stirrings of annoyance churned in his gut.

She trailed the backs of her fingers down the center of his chest, to his torso, his navel, then stopped. "Control doesn't even enter into this discussion."

She plucked at the line of hair arrowing down low on his belly. "You're a very sexy man, Jace Morgan. A very sexual man. I just don't see you doing without."

Stark honesty replaced annoyance. "Sex hasn't been an issue with me for a very long time."

A light blush pinkened her cheeks, so out of character for the woman who'd just blown his socks off.

"Don't you get . . . frustrated?"

He smiled at her candor, and the fact that her fingers had drifted lower. "Sure, the same as any healthy adult."

"So what do you do about it?"

Lifting a brow and wondering how much honesty Eden could take, Jace finally shrugged. "I work it off."

"The weight bench?"

"Or an ax and a log. Maybe a band saw. Or a plane. The small jobs sap me mentally. When my brain shuts down, my body seems to do the same." He budged up a bit, helping her fingers along on a quest that was taking entirely too long.

Eden's sigh drifted over his skin like the barest breeze. "Three years is a long time to go it alone."

Elbows propped on the stair above where Eden reclined, Jace sat on the one below. Their matched breathing and the slurp and slosh of water made the only sound in the room.

As silences went, this one was suddenly too depressing. He leaned out and flipped on the Jacuzzi.

The motor droned and the jet of bubbles sent awareness skating over his skin. Or maybe it was Eden's foot skimming the length of his lower leg that was heating the heated water.

Either would work, as long as he didn't have to think about tomorrow. About the fact that this had probably been a mistake. About how two people with the type of intimate knowledge he and Eden shared were supposed to go back to being just friends.

Which they'd have to do. Because they certainly had no future.

"I saw the wall, Jace. The pictures hanging there. They're very elegantly framed. And evenly spaced. Did you realize they're hanging in three exact rows of six?"

He heaved a thought-filled sigh. And now, of course, she was gonna want to talk about it. "Not only do I design, I decorate."

She took a deep breath, raised her chin and

glanced at the ceiling, then back down at her hand on his stomach, her foot on his leg.

And Jace just rolled his eyes and waited for it.

"How can you be satisfied hanging kitchen cabinets? Building shelves and rocking chairs? Running electrical wires for dances you don't want to attend?"

He shrugged. "I like what I do. I like my life."

"This isn't your life." She slapped the water, splashing his face. "Your life is on that wall."

Irritation boiled through him and Jace jabbed an equally exasperated finger in the air. "What's on that wall are pieces of paper covered with pencil scratches. My life is downstairs in the shop."

"Fine." She crossed her arms over her chest and leaned back. Three minutes later, she came back with, "Did you design this bath?"

He knew it. She wasn't going to let it go. Give him two dogs and one bone any day over tenacious Eden Karr.

"No. I stole it from one of the designers who worked in the same firm I used to. Figured I'd make some good use of the space up here."

"Or so you say."

"What is that supposed to mean?"

"I know you better than that, Jace Morgan. You built this hedonistic, decadent bath because you couldn't stand not having a visual, life-size reminder of what you were born to do. What you love to do."

Jace puffed up his cheeks and blew out a gust of air. He didn't want to fight. He didn't want to argue. He didn't want to admit to himself how right she was.

So he scooped her up caveman style and settled her across his lap. "Why do we have to get into this now?"

"Into what?" she asked, playing the innocent as effectively as she'd played the wanton. What he didn't like was her playing analyst. Or not thinking he had the smarts to catch on.

"You knew who I was when you came here tonight, Eden. And I hope you didn't come here thinking that you can change me."

The fact that she tried to hide her face in her shoulder was a dead giveaway. "You're not my therapist, Eden. What you are is my lover."

"For now, yes. But what about tomorrow? What about ten tomorrows from now?"

He kissed her. "I can't tell you squat about ten tomorrows from now. Ten tomorrows from now you might be living the rat race back in New York."

She pushed against his shoulders, leaning back. "So this is all that matters to you? Here and now?"

Resignation followed sadness through her eyes, the lifeless green a shade he'd never seen. What he saw in her eyes—the hopelessness, the surrender— ate away at the tenuous hold he had on the present.

And it scared him.

Didn't she know he couldn't even think about a future, no matter how much he might wish it? That he wouldn't want a long-distance relationship if she returned to New York, and that he sure wasn't going to follow her there should she go?

She caressed his jaw, spread her thumb across his spiky lashes. "What happened to taking chances?"

Not tonight. No more tonight. He already felt like he'd been flayed and his skin sandpapered on the inside. Ecstasy had left him as raw emotionally as physically.

He couldn't think of tonight as a beginning. He *refused* to think of tonight as a beginning. It was only one night, one time. "Please, Eden. Give me tonight."

A tender smile graced her lips and she swiped the moisture from her eyes. Pushing him back in a prone position, she climbed aboard, bracing her hands on either side of his head as she held tight to the edge of the tub.

The water buoyed her body. As warm as the water was, it didn't compare to her inner heat; as wet as it was, it didn't match her dewy moisture. He'd be lucky to last ten minutes.

Make that five, he silently amended, giving himself up.

She moved against him, rubbing, grinding, riding high, then sliding low. He kissed whatever skin he could reach and floated beneath her, caught between the pull of her body and the need to drive deep, touching softly, not touching at all.

He was drunk with wanting her. His hands hovered over her body, the water lapping in erotic waves, kissing places he wanted to kiss, licking intimately at her skin.

Being buried within her wasn't enough. He wanted to open her fully and crawl inside. Wrap himself up and pretend that, tomorrow, this *would* be enough.

She leaned forward, nipped at his skin, her impatience rising with his. He shifted slightly, his feet finding support on the lowest step. Knees bent, he thrust upward.

Then his surging slowed in speed and became grace and power. He answered her cries with his body.

Her contractions ripped him, shredded him with pleasure, and he spilled into her once again, wishing he could give her more than this fleeting bit of himself, wishing he could give her all his tomorrows.

Jace reached for her in the middle of the night. Exhausted and almost dry, they'd finally made it to bed, though the futon wasn't quite the bed he'd imagined sharing with her.

And while she slept, he kissed her, loving her with tender strokes of his tongue, sharper tugs of his lips.

He curled around her, lying awake long past the time her breathing evened and slowed. He spent that time with her babies, feeling them kick and shove and punch her too-tight skin.

And he prayed she didn't hear him when he whispered, "I wish I'd known you before, Eden. I wish these babies were mine."

When he woke in the morning, she was gone.

Eden glanced at the clock on the wall one more time and groaned, the sound loud enough for the eight customers milling The Fig Leaf to hear. Of course, none of them did.

They were too wrapped up in their shopping to realize that the shop closed in ten minutes. At least on Sundays she didn't open until noon and had the luxury of closing early at five. The way she was feeling today, she never would've lasted her usual nine to six.

She was exhausted and emotionally empty, another fact no one around her seemed to have picked up on. Which was probably a good thing. If she looked half as bad as she felt, no one would have dared to venture inside. Which probably wasn't a good thing at all.

For as badly as she wanted to usher everyone out, crawl upstairs and into bed, she knew she'd made enough money today to make up for a week's worth of slow days down the road. And right now that mattered more than anything.

Even so, all she'd managed to do was stay balanced on her stool, speak the appropriate words at the appropriate times, hopefully make correct change and lift a pencil when somebody asked for a receipt.

What kind of craziness had come over her last night? Why had she kidded herself about the reason she'd gone to his barn? So far, she'd prided herself on her handling of the major changes in her life. So when had her relationship with Jace become so unmanageable?

Try when she fell in love.

And that had happened . . . when? When she'd danced with him under The Emporium's spreading oak? When she'd come apart in his arms that night in the truck? How about when he'd replaced the chime above her door? Or when he'd helped her down off her kitchen counter?

No. If there was one single moment that was a turning point in her life, it was the first moment she'd seen him, when he'd picked up that baby blanket and torn apart her image of what made a man a man.

An image sealed when he'd stroked her in the middle of the night and wished he'd created her babies with his love.

"Excuse me, ma'am?"

Eden blinked twice before focusing on the woman standing at the counter.

"There's no price on this blanket. Could you tell me what you're asking for it?" She handed Jace's blanket across the counter.

As evenly as she could manage, Eden reached out to close trembling fingers around the delicately woven threads. She clutched the blanket to her chest; her throat swelled shut and her emotional stamina dissolved.

"I'm sorry," she whispered. "This blanket isn't for sale. Perhaps I can help you select another."

The woman lifted both shoulders, her pinched mouth a grimace as she sighed. "I don't think so, dear. I didn't see another suitable item."

Eden's swallowed her frustration. "Then I'm sure you won't mind turning the sign to CLOSED on your way out."

Chin in the air, the woman wheeled around, her

gold mules slapping indignant steps across the floor. The door eased closed behind her and Eden jammed her hands over her ears, the music of Jace's chime singing of his compassion and his care.

When she next looked up she found herself alone. She climbed from the stool, plodded to the front door and, for the first time since she'd lived in Arbor Glen, flipped the lock. No one, not even Molly Hansen or Chloe Angelino, was going to disturb her much needed cry.

Whether due to hormones or sadness or weeks of stress, she needed the release of long, quiet tears. But they wouldn't come. She stood there in the silent minutes after closing, while the clock ticked, while the old house shifted and settled, and the tears refused to come. Fine, she thought miserably, and stomped one foot.

And now, on top of everything else, she'd come home in the early hours of the morning to find two messages on her machine. Desperate messages. One from the woman who'd been her administrative assistant at *Elite Woman* magazine and the other from the magazine's publisher.

They wanted her back. They needed her back. They were willing to pay anything to have her come back. That *anything* included flexible hours to accommodate her parenting needs, as well as on-site day care. Private, individualized day care in a room adjacent to her office.

The offer had hit all her buttons, and now she had the biggest decision of her life to make. Did she go? Or did she stay?

Her back door banged open; the screen whacked shut behind. Tools clattered, metal ringing against metal, like dumped from one box to another. The slamming doors echoed in reverse, like whoever—*be honest, Eden*—like Jace was leaving.

She breathed deep, wondering whether he was coming back, whether he wanted to see her, whether she had the strength to move.

Pushing off the front door, she made her way to the kitchen just as Jace came back inside, rocking chair in hand.

He hadn't shaved, and his face appeared haggard and drawn beneath a scruffy growth of dark whiskers, his eyes the dull blue of exhaustion. He wore black from head to toe. But still he smiled.

"You forgot what you came for." He set the rocker in motion with the toe of his moccasin.

"Thanks. But you didn't need to make a special trip."

"Why not? You made a special trip last night. You didn't even wake me up to help you load it this morning." He propped lazy hands on his hips. "I figured it was the least I could do to drop it by."

She wasn't going to tell him that she'd completely forgotten about the rocking chair. "You were sleeping so soundly, I didn't want to wake you."

"I slept like a baby." He stretched and yawned, obviously trying to convince her. Too bad his eyes lied. "You look like you could use a few more hours."

She laughed lightly. If he only knew. "Believe me, I plan to do all I can to catch up tonight."

"Well," he began, rubbing a palm over the back of his neck, "the festival's over. Tomorrow the shops are closed. You ought to climb into bed, unplug the phone and sleep until Tuesday morning."

She wondered if she'd be able to sleep alone, after knowing the joy of sleeping with him. She was going to have to get over that, though. Especially since he refused to talk about tomorrow.

"That sounds like a smart thing to do." Show time. "I wish I'd thought to unplug my phone last night."

He frowned. "Why's that?"

"I got a call from New York." She hoped her voice sounded as casual as she was working for. She held up two fingers. "Two calls actually."

He nodded slowly. "They've offered you the moon to come back, haven't they?"

"Close enough."

"Are you going?" he asked, his jaw tight.

"I don't know. I thought I'd take at least thirty-six hours to think on it."

"You're done with the spur of the moment decisions, huh?"

"I've had mixed luck with those. Hiring you on the spot was one of the better ones."

"And shopping for a rocking chair in the middle of the night was one of the worst."

"Not worst. Just not smartest." Hmm. That hadn't come out exactly the way she'd intended. "What I meant was—"

"I know what you meant, Eden. We both have a

lot going on right now. And neither one of us needs the complication of a relationship."

She nodded. "You're right."

"I mean, I'm not even going to be much of a friend for the next few months." Jace began to pace. "I've promised the Browns to have The Glen finished by Labor Day. They've even given me use of a spare bedroom. I doubt I'll be going home but every couple of days to check on Chelsea.

"I wanted to come by and tell you that, so you wouldn't think I was avoiding you or anything. I mean, after last night I wasn't sure what . . ."

"I wouldn't think that, Jace. I know how important your work is to you. No such thing as too many lines on a résumé." Besides, keeping busy guarantees you won't have time to make friends who you might later fail.

"Speaking of that résumé," he said and raised a finger. "I have one other thing I need to give you. Hang on. I'll be right back." He left through the back door but returned before Eden even found the time to catch her breath.

Of course, there was really no need to catch it, not when she was sure she'd forgotten how to breathe. Her heart seized fast in her chest as Jace set two cradles, identical to the one she'd seen in his shop, on her kitchen table.

With the barest touch of a finger, he placed one in motion. She wanted to tell him thank you. She wanted to tell him she loved him. She wanted him to want her, to need her to stay.

But he didn't even give her a chance to say a word.

He just leaned forward, kissed her cheek and whispered, "I'll see you soon." He was gone before she'd even looked away from the cradles.

And once he left she finally found the strength to cry.

The Glen's Grand Opening was held the last Saturday in August, a week before the proposed date for completion the Browns had given Jace.

The residents of Arbor Glen had been invited to a Friday-night buffet, where Paul conducted tours and Leah offered everyone a free night of lodging complete with complimentary breakfast.

The gesture of goodwill was in part an appreciation of the residents' support of the historic restoration. But Eden knew it was more.

It was a gesture of good business. If everyone in town told two friends and they told two friends and so on and so on and so on, the Browns would soon be booked solid.

Eden had planned to attend the open house with Tucker and Molly but had ended up driving out alone. She'd been caught with a last-minute story deadline and needed to fax off the proofed pages.

Since that first desperate contact with the *Elite Woman* Magazine staff three months ago, Eden had appeased the career gods by agreeing to a series of articles—as much to keep her foot in the door as anything.

She still hadn't made a final decision about her future. But between the freelance work she was doing for the magazine and the incredible business she was doing at The Fig Leaf, she'd barely found time to sleep.

And now she'd run out of time. The twins were due in two weeks and, for the moment, she could think of nothing else but the advent of motherhood.

She'd seen Jace on the streets of Arbor Glen, but never to stop and talk to. A time or two he'd looked like he had something to say, but then he'd waved and moved on.

It was just as well. She wasn't going to make any progress toward the future if she continued to hang on to any part of her past.

Standing at the foot of The Glen's staircase, Eden came to a complete stop. That's what she was doing, wasn't it? Hanging on to her past.

She hadn't let go of New York. She hadn't let go of the magazine. If she had, she wouldn't be killing herself with the articles.

And she hadn't even let go of Jace. Here she was, on the precipice of motherhood—not to mention owning an amazingly profitable and fulfilling business—and she hadn't cut the apron strings binding her to the past.

She laughed once. Twice. And then she pulled out imaginary scissors and snipped.

"Eden? I'd like you to meet some friends of mine."

Eden turned at the sound of Jace's voice. He looked absolutely wonderful, wearing khaki Dockers and a crisp white oxford cloth shirt. "Hello, Jace. You're looking well."

"Thanks. I am well. And you're . . ." His wide-eyed gaze landed on her belly.

"Due," she filled in.

His smile was tender and loving and gave rise to so many questions she wanted to ask. But most of all, she wanted to tell him of her discovery. That here, standing in the house he'd restored, everything had fallen into place.

"I was going to say overdue, but I'll take your word for it." He turned to his side then, to the three men there talking. "Eden, these are my friends. This is Kevin and Robert and Marv. The guys I told you about. They came to celebrate my unveiling."

"And this time he even showed up," Kevin said, then ducked Jace's imaginary punch.

"I'm so pleased to meet you. To meet all of you." Her gaze traveled among the three men. "Jace told me about the soccer team and about the prom and . . . well, I'm probably getting him in trouble here, aren't I?"

Jace raised one brow. "I think you've said enough. But that's okay, because I told them about your appetite."

This time Robert deflected Eden's jab, stepping between her and Jace. "What he really told us about was your cooking."

Marv stepped in to interrupt, a hopeful expression on his face. "Shrimp Creole, I think he said?"

"And I see *you* haven't changed a bit, still haggling for free meals." Arms crossed, Jace shook his head and imitated Molly's tsk-tsk.

Eden had never seen Jace this happy. Had never

seen him with such a carefree expression. And she'd never realized how very very, much she loved this man.

And as she stood there and witnessed the reunion of old friends, Eden's water broke.

"Shh, baby. It's okay. You're doing fine. We're almost there."

Jace's words filtered down to Eden's ears. Regardless of her determination to show a brave front, she dug her fingers into the steel of his thighs.

The muscles of her abdomen pulled fast, tightening over her distended belly like wet leather left in the sun. It hurt. Oh, God, it hurt. Like nothing she'd ever known. She'd never pay attention to a new-mother magazine again.

Even her quick, rhythmic, blowing pants couldn't stop the moans building in her throat. When the pain ended, she collapsed and let her head loll onto Jace's shoulder, awaiting the next contraction.

One hand on the wheel, Jace brushed her tangled hair from her face before checking her middle with his broad palm. His caress was rough but tender. Irritating. Comforting.

She wanted him to stroke her forever. She wanted him to keep his hands to himself. Confusion reigned until she was certain of only one thing.

She wanted Jace by her side.

"How much longer?" she asked, her voice grating against her raw throat. She needed a drink of water.

She needed to get drunk. Then she wouldn't feel a thing.

"Ten minutes. Fifteen tops." Jace wrapped his arm around her shoulder, pulling her close to his side.

She grimaced. Then groaned. Another spasm ripped through her. Concentrate. Focus. She stared at the volume knob of the truck's radio, listened to the low bass of Jace's voice. Nothing helped. She tightened her hand on his thigh and squeezed.

When the storm subsided, she collapsed like a rag doll minus the stuffing. "What time is it now?"

He checked his watch. "They're coming every seven minutes. One more and we'll be at the hospital."

"Oh, Jace. I can't wait that long. Just stop the truck. I'll have the babies here."

Jace chuckled. "That's my girl."

His words were sweet music. She wanted to be his girl. Wanted to be his everything. Fighting back a rush of fear, she begged, "Jace, stay with me."

"Every minute of the way."

She marginally relaxed, and even though she hadn't meant to beg she'd give up her right arm before she'd take back a word. "I didn't mean to take you away from your friends."

"Don't worry, Eden." His voice was soft and loving. A lover's voice. "You didn't take me away from anything."

Six-and-a-half minutes of silence later, the next contraction sliced through her. Perspiration soaked the back of her blouse.

Sweat ran down her forehead and she squeezed

her eyes shut over the salty burn. When they pulled into the emergency entrance, Eden whimpered.

Heedless of blocking the drive, Jace whipped open his door and scooped her into his arms. She buried her face in his neck and exhaled in short, sharp, agonizing pants.

"Hang on, Eden." He mumbled the encouragement into her hair. His long strides carried them through the sliding glass doors. Sterile smells of pine and antiseptic soap swirled around. Running steps squeaked and thudded on the tiled floor.

"Sir! Stop, please." The deep voice commanded attention.

Muttering a low curse, Jace shot a quick glance over his shoulder.

"Sir, you can't leave your truck in the drive like that."

Eden saw only a gunbelt and a starched blue uniform before the next squeezing cramp ripped her in two. "Jace!"

"Park it. I'll be in maternity." Jace flipped his keys to the security officer before banging through the swinging metal doors into the maternity ward.

Inside, order reigned supreme. Jace settled Eden into a wheelchair and she whimpered. She couldn't sit. The pressure on her lower body shot to the top of her head.

A crisply efficient obstetric nurse wheeled her into a labor room. Scared, feeling abandoned, and hurting beyond words, she reached back.

She needed Jace.

The nurse patted her shoulder and leaned down

to whisper in a low, calming voice, "Don't worry,
Mrs. Karr. He's no more than three feet behind like
a good man should be. Now, let's get these babies
delivered so you can see your feet again."

Eden managed a weak smile and then a groan as
the nurse stopped the chair next to a table and laid
a hospital gown on the end. No way.

She couldn't stand up. She couldn't get out of her
clothes. She couldn't climb up there. But somehow
she did all three, then collapsed back onto the rock-
hard pillow.

After a quick prep and exam, the nurse pro-
claimed Eden well on her way to motherhood, then
left to call the doctor, thrusting a set of scrubs at
Jace on her way out.

He took a tentative step into the room, gesturing
with the hospital greens. "I guess she thinks I'm the
father."

Pushing up on her elbows, breathing hard, Eden
said, "You don't have to do this, you know."

"Are you kidding? Only a fool would pass up a
chance like this."

She reached for his hand, groaned and panted.
Jace swabbed the sweat from her forehead with a
cool cloth.

"You doin' okay?"

She nodded, grunted, and rubbed her tongue
over her dry lips. "You'd better see if the doctor's
decided to put in an appearance."

Jace bolted out the door, and the next thing Eden
knew, a battalion of attendants descended, shifting
monitors and IV bottles for the trip to delivery.

Once inside all she felt was cold, but not enough to numb the pain. Transition hit hard, and she barely recovered from one contraction before the next struck.

She existed in a pain-racked nightmare, the doctor between her legs, the nurses hovering close by and Jace at her head, brushing the hair from her forehead. Her fingers bit into the sheet at her sides.

"Okay, Eden. Let's get cracking." Dr. Tremont leveled her kindly gaze on Eden, her gray eyes crinkling at the corners. The look she pinned on Jace wasn't kindly at all. "Glad to see you could make it for the final event, Dad."

"He's not—" Eden began, before Jace cut her off.

"Shh, baby. Save your breath."

"Dad's right," Dr. Tremont interrupted, her tone no-nonsense and firm. "This little fella doesn't have time to argue. When I count to three, push for all you're worth. Ready? One. Two. Three."

Pressing up on her elbows with Jace's arm to support her, Eden grunted. And pushed. And groaned until the contraction passed. Drained, she collapsed against the table.

Less than a minute later, Dr. Tremont quietly commanded, "Let's do it again."

And she did, pressing back against Jace as she bore down, and down, and down. Her cries echoed off the walls.

"That's it, Eden. Once more and you'll be a mother." The nurse to the right dabbed the sweat from the doctor's brow.

Jace did the same for Eden. Opening her eyes,

she looked directly into his, red-rimmed yet full of the love he vehemently denied.

Her own eyes welled in response, but before she could think any further her baby demanded her full attention.

Please, please, let this be all. Another push. Another groan. And baby number one slid into the doctor's hands.

Eden dropped back on the table. "Who is it?"

Jace turned to the nurse attending the crying infant. She finished, laying the swaddled bundle in Jace's arms. "Here Dad. Hold your daughter while we finish up with Mom and number two."

Bethany.

Standing near Eden's head, Jace stroked the infant's cheek, ear and nose. The baby quieted, Jace looked up and Eden saw in his gaze a father's love, love born in commitment and caring.

In that moment, she knew she would love him forever.

"Jace," she managed to whisper, "do you mind showing me my daughter before I get too busy to look?"

"Oh, Eden. She's gorgeous." Jace laid the tiny bundle across Eden's chest.

Bethany was no bigger than the soft-sculpted dolls Eden sold in her shop. A dusting of mahogany hair feathered over her head.

Eden nuzzled her lips across the tiny fist and swept one finger down her daughter's ruddy red cheek. Tears matted her lashes as she looked up at Jace.

"She *is* gorgeous."

"Just like her mother." Jace brushed his lips across hers with an air of possession.

The doctor cleared her throat at the same time Eden groaned. "There'll be time for that later, Dad. Let's get baby number two out of the way first. Nurse." Dr. Tremont gave a quick nod, and the nurse swept Bethany from Eden's chest.

She felt the loss of the tiny weight as acutely as the pain knifing through her lower body. Then she felt Jace at her shoulder, muttering low words of encouragement and bracing her back as she strained.

Five minutes and three pushes later, Benjamin entered the world. Exhausted and numb, Eden suffered through the final procedures and watched through heavy-lidded eyes as the obstetrical team cleaned up her son, again handing the bundle to Jace.

"I'll give the four of you about ten minutes to get acquainted, then these babies are off to the nursery and Mrs. Karr to recovery." Returning Bethany to Eden's chest, the interrupting nurse gave Jace a stern look. "Ten minutes."

At last they were alone. Eden gulped down a huge breath. She glanced from her squirming red-faced daughter to her purple-splotched son to the man at her side, the man she loved.

She had so much to say but no strength to talk or energy to order her thoughts. Exhaling long and slow, she found herself fighting to keep her eyes from drifting shut. Of all the stinking timing.

"Do you want me to call the nurse?"

Eden's lids fluttered open. She smiled weakly and

shook her head. "I think I can manage ten minutes without passing out."

Her gaze traveled from the blanket-wrapped bundle wiggling in Jace's arms to the similar one nuzzling her chest. Anxiety and anticipation weighed heavy on her mind, but nothing could push away the overwhelming love.

"Oh, Jace, they're perfect. Absolutely beautiful."

"You did a hell of a job, Mom." Jace cleared his throat and swiped a knuckle across one eye, then laid Ben next to Beth on Eden's chest, cradling them both in the crook of his elbow.

"Okay, Mrs. Karr," the nurse with impeccable timing called from the doorway. Marching into the icy delivery room, she scooped both wrapped bundles from Eden's chest. "Let's get these babies settled in and you cleaned up."

"Jace . . ."

"Shh." Alone again, he brushed the hair back from Eden's face. "You get some rest."

Closing her fingers around his, she brought his hand to her mouth, kissing each finger, then pressing her lips to the center of his palm. "How can I ever say thank you?"

"You just did." He repeated the gentle caress, then lowered his head.

Eden closed her eyes and gave herself up, opening her lips to accept the pillow-soft pressure of his. Cool and clean, his mouth touched the corners of her mouth. Soft and stubbled, his chin grazed hers. Warm and damp, his breath breezed against her upper lip.

A loud clearing of a throat penetrated Eden's fog. Jace lifted his head and, bereft of his warmth, the shakes set in.

In two steps the nurse was at her side, tucking the blanket around her shoulders before unlocking the wheels on the bed. "C'mon, Mom. It's recovery for you."

"Wait," Eden managed to order between chattering teeth. "Jace?"

He squeezed her shoulder, her arm, her hand, and trailed his fingers from the tips of hers.

"Good-bye, Eden."

TWELVE

Propped back on a stack of pillows, Eden nuzzled first Ben's head, then moved her lips to Beth's. Baby scent and sweet skin and the downy softness of newborn hair. Was there anything more precious?

She remembered then that she'd once measured the preciousness of Chelsea's puppies. Wondered then, too, if she'd had less maternal instinct than Jace's dog. All these months later, the thought was nothing if not silly. Less maternal instinct than a dog? As if.

Resting against her sore breasts, the tiny bodies seemed heavier than their respective four pounds, thirteen ounces and five pounds, two. But Eden wasn't about to complain.

They were here and they were healthy and soon she could once again see her feet and sleep on her stomach. And, naturally, just as she began to doze, the nurse arrived to spirit her new family away.

"I'm sorry, Mrs. Karr, but the pediatrician's due any minute. If I don't get the twins back to the nursery for their final checkup, you may not get out of here today." She scooped up the infants from Eden's chest.

Immediately missing the warmth and the weight, Eden pulled the bedclothes to her chest. "Their gowns are in the top of the closet. Can you get them, or should I?"

"I'll grab them on my way out." The nurse settled the babies side by side in a rolling bassinet, hovering with gentle hands as she adjusted the pink and blue blankets just right. Reaching for the bundle of new clothes, she gave Eden a genuine smile.

"We're going to miss these two. We haven't had twins here since Oneilla May's daughter surprised everyone in the hospital with two seven-pound boys ten years ago."

Before Eden could reply, the nurse was gone, cooing to the twins as the door creaked shut. The squeak-squeal, squeak-squeal of the bassinet wheels faded down the hall.

Eden tossed back the antiseptically stiff sheet and blanket and eased her feet to the floor, wincing at this pinch, yelping at that sting. Reaching for the robe at the end of her bed, she wrapped it tight around her empty body and made her slow way to the window.

The view from her room in the small county hospital was no doubt meant to soothe. But the blinding blue sky and the rolling hills of the tree-dotted horizon had absolutely no numbing effect on Eden's whirring mind.

As dozens of thoughts shifted and settled, one in particular came to a certain rest. She would never regret moving to Arbor Glen; she wouldn't have made the friends she'd made or met Jace otherwise.

The minutes preceding Jace's departure from the delivery room lingered like a haze in her mind. She couldn't account for each second, but she remembered enough.

And for the last two days she'd relived those elusive moments again and again.

After he'd left, after the nurses had wheeled her down one hall, her babies down another, she'd lain alone in her hospital bed, tears of joy and exhaustion soaking the neckline of her hospital-issue gown. She'd been happy and tired; she'd missed Jace sorely.

And she would have liked to give herself a swift kick as a reminder that life wasn't fair. Jace Morgan had never been part of the package. He'd been a sort of bonus. And he'd made no promises of forever.

Her forever was of her own making, and she was preparing for the first step by taking her children home.

To The Fig Leaf.

To Arbor Glen.

At the sharp rap on her door, Eden turned, glad for the interruption. She was daydreaming too much already. And she had *so* much to do now that she'd made her decision to stay and raise her family in Texas. "Yes?"

Molly pushed her way inside, a tapestry bag slung over one shoulder. "Just stopped by the nursery. Had to make sure those precious little ones weren't smothered in blankets. Nothing worse for a newborn than bein' too hot."

Eden stifled a laugh. "And did you find everything to your liking?"

"Ben's face is a wee bit red. Most likely a sensitivity to the laundry soap."

That Molly. Always the mother, Eden mused. "Or maybe he's mad at Bethany for beating him to the punch."

"That could be." Molly tossed the overnighter on the foot of the bed. "I'm afraid I do have some bad news."

"You didn't find Jace."

Molly shook her head. "Tucker and I passed him on Highway 37 headed out toward Stone's place Sunday night. But when Tucker drove back out Monday morning, he found the barn locked up tight. And that fancy showpiece of a truck is missing."

"Well," Eden said with a heavy sigh, "I guess I'll have to find another builder."

"You could wait for Jace to come back," Molly offered.

"I could, but I have no idea how long he'll be gone." Not to mention where he'd disappeared to or why. "And I want to get started on the plans for the new house as soon as I can. I knew the twins and I wouldn't be able to live above The Fig Leaf forever. I just didn't know our rooms would be bursting at the seams this soon."

"Well, I sent Tucker back to straighten out the car seats. You would've thought he'd never belted in dozens of his own grandchildren, looking at the mess he made of the seat belts." Molly snugged an arm around Eden's waist.

Side by side they gazed out the window. "They grow up fast, girl. And before you know it, your two will have children of their own. I've taken care of my share of little ones. And I don't think I could've done it without Tucker around.

"So I want you to promise that any time of the day or night you need me, you'll call."

Eden leaned her head against Molly's and stared at their reflected image, tendrils of her auburn hair brushing the other woman's shoulders. "Oh, Molly. What would I do without you?"

Hiding a sniff in her handkerchief, Molly walked back to the bed and opened the overnighter. She laid out the clothes she'd brought for Eden to wear home. "Don't be worrying about that, because you'll never have to know."

Eden reached for the olive-hued jumper, then took the coordinating mustard-colored blouse from Molly's hands. And then she smiled and began to sing about getting by with a little help from friends.

Jace tossed his pencil to the drafting table, glanced at his watch and stood. He was due to meet Marv for dinner. If he didn't get a move on, he'd be late.

He'd promised himself two things when he'd agreed to help Marv's construction firm by taking on this design job: He would never miss another appointment with a friend and he'd never work late.

Jerking at the knot of his tie, he crossed the width of his temporary office in Houston's Galleria and stared out at the mist rising from the Wall of Water three stories below. When he'd accompanied Marv into his partner's suite deep in The Odyssey Corporation's offices eight weeks ago, one mention of the J. B. Morgan name and he'd had everything he required to do the work handed to him on a silver platter.

He knew the other draftsmen weren't thrilled with his presence. But what they thought didn't concern him. He was here to do a job. One job. For Marv.

The fact that Dennis Perry, Odyssey's VP and Marv's partner, had been receptive to Jace's ideas and had been willing to risk the tempers and hurt feelings of his professional staff barely impacted Jace's performance.

But Marv was counting on him, and for his friend he'd stay—no matter how much he wanted to get back to Arbor Glen. And to Eden.

God, he missed her. He couldn't believe how much. And he couldn't believe he'd floated around in a black hole for so many years. Eden was right—which hadn't really come as a surprise. He'd given up what he was meant to do, and his time here at Odyssey had proven that.

He'd seen a lot in the past eight weeks. Once the Odyssey staff came to grips with the fact that he wasn't after any of their jobs, things around the office had settled into a routine. The sort of routine he was well familiar with. But this time his perspective was way different.

He saw the guys who thought of this as nothing more than a nine to five job, who were out the door before the second hand hit 5:01.

And then he saw the others—the ones he used to be—who remained way after closing, who had families to go home to but chose to stay instead.

He wanted to shake them, knock some sense into them, wake them up so they could see what they were throwing away. His reputation might speak for itself, but other than that . . . well, he hadn't led an exemplary life.

He had no room to talk—even though he wasn't the same man he was when he'd walked out of Dallas three years ago.

The two months he'd spent now in Houston had proved that to his satisfaction. And if he had Eden to come home to every night . . . he couldn't think of a thing that would keep him in the office past closing time. He measured success differently these days.

And the number-one catalyst to his change in thinking had come in that delivery room, when he'd witnessed Eden's two babies entering the world.

He'd seen it in her eyes, felt it in the trembling tips of her fingers, heard it in the shaky hesitation of her voice. She wanted him to stay. Instead, he'd walked. Afraid he'd fail her, that in the end he'd let her down.

But maybe, just maybe, it was way past time he headed in a new direction—even if that direction was the far Northeast. He knew now that he'd survive wherever a life with Eden took him. And knew it well.

"Hell of a concept, Morgan. Hell of a concept."

Darkness had fallen and, in the reflective glass, Jace watched Dennis Perry study the blueprint design laid out on the drafting table. "And it'll do a world of good for public relations."

Jace walked back to the table, looking for what Perry saw. All he could see was what this would mean to Marv. "Yeah, well, not to take anything away from your designers, but sometimes you can make a bigger statement by keeping your mouth shut."

"I like what that says, Morgan. Like it a lot." Perry rubbed at his jaw. His bushy gray brows creased into a frown. "We've got a hell of a design team here, Morgan. A hell of a team. But they're big guns. They can't see the damn trees for the forest. Or the forest for the trees."

He frowned and muttered, "Never have figured out what that means. Anyway, what I'm trying to say is that I've got designers here just as talented as you. It wasn't your name that got you this job. It was the fact that you could see what needed to be done."

"I appreciate your honesty, Mr. Perry."

"Not a problem, Morgan. Not a problem." He slapped Jace on the shoulder, then turned and walked to the door. Pausing, he looked back. "One more thing."

"What's that, sir?"

"I'm off to Galveston with the family for the weekend. And I don't want to see a light burning in this window when I drive by later tonight."

Jace laughed. "Not a chance."

Shaking his head, Perry headed for the door mumbling under his breath. "Kids gotta have their Halloween party on the beach. If that don't beat all, I've ever seen. Eating candy in the sand. What do kids know?" he grumbled, stepped into the hallway, then turned back. "Monday, Morgan. I'll see you Monday and not before."

"Yes, sir. Monday."

Once Perry had gone, Jace reached up and flipped off the halogen lamp. He stared out the window at the taillights and brakelights and headlights of commuters fighting their way home between the 610 Loop and the Southwest Freeway.

He figured he'd give it an hour, let the traffic thin out, then hit the road. He didn't even need to stop at the Westin and pack a bag. He had everything he needed for the weekend back at his barn.

Everything but Eden.

Perched on the edge of the nursery windowseat, Eden stared out the window and up through the branches of the pecan tree toward the sky. Stars blinked in the cloudless sky and the moon shone bright, a perfect trick-or-treat evening.

Eden had never spent a Halloween in Arbor Glen. She'd decorated the front of The Fig Leaf with a row of a dozen carved pumpkins. She was looking forward to the festive night ahead more than she could have imagined when she'd moved here at the beginning of the year.

It was especially poignant since she knew she was home, since she'd come to realize where she lived didn't matter, that the fulfillment she'd been searching for between Texas and New York she'd finally found in her heart.

She still missed Jace. The twins had just turned two months old and she hadn't heard a word from him since the day Beth and Ben had been born. No one seemed to know where he'd gone. Or at least those who might have weren't talking.

She'd seen Stone Healen out behind his shop bathing Chelsea. That had come as a real surprise. Not that Jace had given away his dog, but the fact that he knew somebody well enough to give her to.

Stone hadn't said a word, at least not any that had made any sense. What he'd said had sounded like Latin, except for a cryptic male-bonding remark about a man doing what a man had to do.

Well, whatever Jace had to do, it sure hadn't included her. But that was fine. She'd get along without him. And once he returned, if he did, they'd wrap up their unfinished business and she'd close that chapter of her life. It didn't matter that she loved him.

An incredible ache rose in her throat, one she'd tried to work her way around for the past eight weeks, one she'd tried to ignore, but one that just seemed to hang in her chest, taking pleasure in catching her off guard or at the most inopportune times.

Like every time the chime played when the front door opened and closed. Like every time she reached for a teacup in her new kitchen cabinets. Such as every time she crawled under the covers and spent another night alone.

Good grief, Eden. Just get over it. She was saved from total immersion in self-pity by a snuffling in the cradle behind her. Jace's cradles. She couldn't think of them any other way. Before Ben could fully wake, she hopped up, squatted at his side and patted him back to sleep.

Then, just as she turned to check on Beth, a huge shadow spilled over her from the doorway. She spun around.

"Chloe. You scared me." She pressed a hand to her heart. "What are you still doing here? I thought you left with Molly."

Chloe glided across the room, a tinkle of bells and a swish of skirt the only sound she made. Eden got to her feet just in time to catch the girl as she launched herself forward.

"Oh, Eden. I'm so glad you're going to stay. I just wish Jace were here. It's not cosmically right. The circle isn't complete." Chloe smelled like fresh air and teenaged girl.

Eden hugged her close, marveling at the differences between Chloe and Beth, wondering what her daughter would be like in sixteen years. "You've been a lifesaver these past two months. I don't know how I would've managed without your help in the store every afternoon."

"I can be more help. Nick won't mind. I—"

"Chloe, Nick needs you at home. If I've learned nothing at all in my life, I've learned that one thing.

You have to be there for those closest to you. That's the only way you can be happy with yourself."

"Are you happy with yourself, Eden? Are you happy at last?"

Assuring herself that the twins slept peacefully, Eden guided Chloe back to the windowseat where they sat cross-legged facing each other. "Yes, Chloe, I am. I found what I came here looking for. But I found it in myself. Beth and Ben need *me* more than anything I can give them. And to be the best I can for them *I* have to be happy here."

She gripped Chloe's hand and pressed it between her breasts. "Deep in here. Because when this works, everything works. And I can be the best I can be. Don't ever accept anything less from yourself. And don't ever depend on another person to give you that inner peace."

"Then you didn't find it with Jace?" When Eden didn't answer, Chloe looked down and twisted her skirt in her hands. "I was wrong. I thought you would."

"Jace hasn't found it with himself. If that happens . . ." Eden shrugged. "Who knows? For now I have to think of my babies."

Chloe got to her bare feet and heaved a theatrical sigh. Swiping back loose tendrils of hair and a couple of tears, she said, "I will think of your babies, too. Until I'm old enough to think of my own."

"One more thing," Eden added, climbing down to wrap one arm around Chloe's shoulders and ignoring the teen's wish for babies. "When I finally get settled in the new house, I want you to come to stay for a week. I'll supply the paints and brushes and you can paint your cosmic heart out."

Chloe's eyes widened, and even in the darkened room Eden could see her excitement. Not only did the girl's eyes sparkle like the sun on rain, the suggestion of light hovered from her head to her shoulders.

Eden blinked twice and it was gone, and Chloe was in motion again, enclosing Eden in one last hug. "I will start planning now so I will know the colors when I see them."

Then she was gone in a blur of shadows, but Eden knew she would be all right. Standing at the head of the stairs, she listened for Chloe to go. The barest tinkle of bells reached her ears before the chime rang in the distance. Eden shivered as the song faded away.

And then Bethany's cry of hunger had Eden's breasts filling in automatic response. She reached for her daughter and settled into the rocker—Jace's rocker. Kneading her breast with a tiny fist, Beth nuzzled and rooted as Eden adjusted her blouse.

"Greedy little sister, aren't you?" Eden whispered, sucking in her breath as Beth latched on. She smoothed her palm over Beth's dusting of auburn hair. "Oh, Beth. We'll be just fine, won't we? Just you and me and Ben?"

A quick glance to the cradle at her feet told her that Ben wasn't about to wake up for anything as mundane as eating. No. Her son slept quietly and, knowing Ben, planned to save all his wakeful hours to studying the complexity of his new world.

Eden glanced back at Beth. She gurgled and plopped her fist against the soft swell of Eden's breast. Caressing her daughter's downy head, Eden glanced at the darkened window, the muted lamplight making it a reflective glass.

Resting her head against the back of the rocker, she concentrated on the tiny tugging motions of Beth's mouth until a squeak of the stairs reached her ears. Eden straightened and looked at the glass.

Jace's reflection was clearly outlined in the window, the moonlight illuminating but not defining. She remembered the love in his eyes, the touch of his fingers to hers. But she remembered him best in her heart.

She drank her fill of his blurred image, wishing him into the room but refusing to turn for fear she'd do something stupid like throw herself into his arms. The moment went on.

He was the first to speak. "Hi."

She didn't know where to begin. All she could manage was a return, "Hello."

He came into the room. She followed his approach in the window, though she didn't need to look at all. She felt him under her skin, where his memory had been living for the past endless weeks.

He walked past her and she inhaled, seeking his scent, the one that lingered in the fabric of the jumper she still slept with.

"Chloe let me in on her way out. Something about the timing of the cosmos. Or the alignment of the planets?" His voice slid like liquid sex to the base of her spine.

Trembling, she studied the tense set of his shoulders, the rigid line of his back. He was as affected as she. "You know Chloe."

"Does anyone really know Chloe?" He chuckled softly, intimately, and Eden's soul took flight.

Jace rubbed one hand over the back of his neck, then turned and dropped down on the windowseat. Elbows braced on his widespread knees, he laced his hands and stared at the floor between his feet. "I hear you're looking for a carpenter."

"You can't be a carpenter. I don't see any sweat or sawdust. And you're not wearing those pants with hammers and tape measures hung everywhere."

He patted his pockets, front and rear, coming up with a single nail. He balanced it head down on the window ledge. "Will that do?"

Eden searched for the words she wanted to say, words to complete this full circle without losing any of the ground she'd gained in getting on with her life.

Rubbing a finger across Beth's brow, Eden watched her daughter's hungry cheeks move in and out and decided simple honesty was best. "Did you come for the holiday festivities?"

"That, and to talk."

"To talk?" she whispered, still staring at Beth, though she saw only Jace, felt only Jace, as he moved into her peripheral vision.

When at last she looked up, she found his gaze riveted on the child nursing at her breast. She held her breath, her heart pounding.

Hands shoved deep in the pockets of his jeans, he

remained silent, shifting slightly to stare down at Ben in his cradle.

Eden longed for brighter light to see Jace's face. But the shadows made it impossible, so she waited, watching while he leaned down and, with one broad hand, stroked Ben's back.

"I can't believe he's so tiny," he whispered, measuring Ben's width between his outstretched fingers.

Eden smiled. "Most of what you see there is diapers."

He looked up, and the barest of twinkles shimmered in his eyes, sparkling brighter when he dropped his gaze to Beth. He took two steps, sank to his knees at Eden's feet and raised his hand.

She arched back, and the sudden movement jerked her nipple from Beth's hold. The baby whimpered, and Jace, using his finger as a lead, guided Beth's tiny mouth back to its source of nourishment.

His hand lingered, the backs of his fingers stroking across the swell of her blue-veined skin. Leaning forward, he dropped a kiss on Beth's downy head, and Eden thought she would die.

"Am I too late, Eden?" He whispered the words against the baby's head.

"Too late for what?"

His gaze roamed from her eyes to her breast and back. "For you and me."

Taking a step she knew she would never regret, she brushed back his hair with her fingers and cupped his jaw in her palm. "I don't know. What time is it?"

"What?"

She shook her head. "No, Jace. You're not too late. You're never too late. I love you."

His eyes filled with tears and he glanced away quickly. Eden's gaze followed his as he looked down at Beth. Dribbles of milk ran from the sleeping baby's open mouth to her chin.

"I don't know why you should."

"Jace—"

"No, let me finish." He dabbed at Beth's chin with the pad of his thumb, rubbing the milky residue into his palm. "I walked out on you at the hospital. I knew I couldn't stay and give you what you needed."

"And now?" She held her breath, not wanting to miss a word.

He raised his searching gaze to hers. "Now I know that I'm one hell of a selfish man."

"Why do you say that?"

"Because I want you, and I'm too mercenary to let you go. Even if I have to follow you to New York—"

"I'm not going to New York."

"Ever?"

"Ever." She swallowed. Hard.

Smiling, Jace went on, stroking his palm over Beth's head. "Whether you ever want another child or not, I'll be a damned good father to these two."

"Jace . . ."

"I'll be a good husband and provider."

"Jace . . ."

"And I want you enough that whether or not we have children together doesn't really matter."

Laying her fingers across his lips, Eden interrupted a third time. "Jace?"

He took her fingers in his, kissing the tip of each one. "I love you, Eden."

She lowered her head and brushed her lips across first one eye, then the other. "I love you, too. But I'm a very selfish woman."

"How do you figure?"

"The thought of bearing your children thrills me. Except for the labor pains part." She grinned. "But what I want is you. You only. You first. You. Always and forever."

Eyes closed, Jace lowered his head, his lashes brushing butterfly kisses against her skin. He laid his face against the fullness of her breast and breathed deeply, his warm breath wafting across her milk-wet nipple.

When he opened his mouth, Eden shuddered all the way to her soul. His tongue traced the veins spidering across her skin from one slope to the other and down toward the dusky center. He skipped over it, instead placing a feather-light kiss on Beth's mouth. The baby wiggled and Eden's eyes filled with tears.

Threading her fingers through Jace's thick hair, she tugged, pulling him close. Silken and mercurial, a sliver of longing shimmied to the base of her spine, erupting in a maelstrom of desire far beyond the physical.

This man was made to be her other half.

He lifted his head. "Eden Karr," he began, his voice a husky shade of gravel, "will you do me the honor of becoming my wife, my only lover and the mother of my children?"

She saw the reflection of her smile in his eyes. "I'll be your everything."

Jace eased the sleeping baby from her mother's arms and laid her in her cradle. In another equally fluid move, he had Eden on her feet and in his arms, his pale eyes ghostly bright. "I'm yours forever."

"I love you, Jace," Eden whispered. She buried her face in his chest, then just as quickly looked up. "Where have you been? I've been out of my mind—"

"Later." He nuzzled her neck, his hands making short work of her half-fastened bra.

"Molly's waiting for me to call. I need—"

"Later."

"Jace, I don't have any furniture. We can't—"

"Yes. We can." Her blouse drifted to the floor. Jace's shirt followed. "We have moonlight—"

"But—"

"And we have each other."

EPILOGUE

"Mommy! Mommy!" Her nearly three-year-old legs pumping as fast as chubby muscles and training pants allowed, Beth ran with wild abandon down the grassy drive. Ignoring his sister's undignified behavior, Ben followed three paces behind.

Eden stepped from the passenger-side of Molly's station wagon just in time to intercept her daughter. Catching the toddler on the run, Eden swung Beth up and around while she squealed her delight.

"Hey, little sister. Are you ready to go with Grandma Molly?" She gave Beth's nose an Eskimo kiss, then glanced down to find Ben tugging at her skirt. "And just look at little brother. Don't you look handsome."

"Handsome," Ben echoed, smoothing down his blue-and-red western shirt. "Daddy says handsome too."

Eden scooped Ben up in her other arm. "That daddy of yours has good taste."

She smacked her son on the cheek, tossing a quick glance over Ben's mahogany curls in time to see Jace

shoulder open the screened porch door, a pint-size
suitcase in each hand.

Her heart tripped into a tailspin. One whole night.
An entire night with her husband. Just her and Jace,
no rambunctious two-year-olds pleading for endless
bedtime stories and one more drink. Thank good-
ness for Molly Hansen.

Beth caught sight of her adoptive grandmother.
"Grandma Mo-lly!"

Eden let her daughter slide to the ground. Beth
had barely touched down before she was climbing
through the open door of the station wagon, over
the front seat and into one of the car seats Molly
kept in the back.

Hands on her hips, Molly shook her head. "No
question but that girl's ready to go." She took a step
toward Eden, holding out her arms to Ben. "How
about you, young man?"

Ben promptly and wetly kissed his mother on the
mouth, then dived from her arms to Molly's.

This time it was Eden who laughed. "It's a good
thing my feelings don't hurt easily or I'd think those
two preferred your company to mine."

"Of course they do. They've got me wrapped
around their pinkies." Molly buckled Beth into the
car seat and leaned across to do the same for Ben.
"You two want to tell your mother good-bye?"

Identical hands waved, and both toddlers blew
sloppy kisses. One reserved and one boisterous voice
shouted, "Bye-bye."

Molly shot Eden a triumphant grin. "Ah, the joys

of being a grandmother. I can spoil them rotten, then bring them home."

"Thank you so very much," Eden quipped. "Maybe Jace and I will decide not to pick them up this time. How do you like them apples?"

"You forget, girl, I know where you live." Molly narrowed one teasing eye.

"Are you talking about fruit or my babies?" Jace tossed the suitcases into the front seat and leaned over to kiss the twins. He tickled Beth, ruffled Ben's hair and both giggled in delight.

Eden's heart swelled. From day one of their marriage Jace had accepted the twins as his own. He'd diapered, rocked, fed and burped, paced the floor and crooned to Ben, who'd been the only one to suffer colic.

He was an indestructible tower of patience, spending time with Ben building cities out of blocks, time with Beth dressing and undressing dolls. And time showing Eden passion unlike any she'd ever known. Nothing could make their lives any more perfect.

But there was one little thing that might just be the icing on the cake.

Drawing her close to his side, Jace wrapped his arm around her shoulder, and together they watched Molly's car disappear over the hill. "You and Molly have a good time at the meeting? The historic society decide on a new project for me to save?"

"Of course we had a good time. Of course we're working on finding you a project. But the best part of all is walking through The Glen, showing off your talent and telling everyone that I sleep with the man responsible for the design."

Jace scowled. "You do not."

Smiling, Eden snuggled closer to the warmth she never wanted to lose. She buried her face against Jace's side and breathed deeply of the man she loved.

"What's that all about?"

She grinned into his shirt, then slipped away and jogged up the porch steps. "Do I need a reason?"

Jace followed, catching the screen door before it slammed in his face. "Seems you don't need a reason for anything today. You gonna tell me why you had Molly take the kids?"

"So we can celebrate."

"Celebrate what?"

"Nothing much. Just being in love."

"You call that nothing much?" he called from the entrance to the hall.

Eden strolled its length, dropping first her purse, then her sweater, then her blouse in a provocative trail.

"Eden, what the hell are you doing?"

"You complaining, Morgan?" She disappeared into their bedroom. After tossing her bra out the door, then her jeans, then her panties, she added in a sultry voice, "Or are you coming?"

"Is that an invitation?" he growled from the doorway, adding his clothes to the pile.

"Since when have you needed one?"

Her chin propped in her palms, her crossed ankles swinging side to side, Eden lay on her stomach on their bed. Waiting. Wanting. Wildly in love.

Her gaze swept the length of her husband's naked body, coming to rest at a point several inches below his navel. She wet her lips once, twice, catching the lower between her teeth as her eyes drifted shut.

Jace groaned. Two seconds and two long steps later, and with the symmetry only longtime lovers share, his body covered hers, his mouth doing the same, needlessly seeking her surrender. Like the rarest of orchids in a gardener's hands, she blossomed beneath him, opening, welcoming, calling him home.

Their movements choreographed, their hearts pounding in syncopated rhythm, their blood pulsing to fulfill matching desire, Eden and Jace loved. And she knew no single being could boast the perfection found in the oneness they shared.

Eden pressed back against the mattress, arching her hips to take Jace completely. Her legs around his hips, her arms encircling his neck, she rode the storm, a tempest made fierce by the intensity of their love. The lightning flashed. The thunder rolled. And savoring each and every tempestuous moment, Eden climbed to the peak.

"C'mon, baby, do it." Jace growled the command against her neck, forcing her higher. He nipped fiercely at her throat. She twisted and moaned. Hands beneath her hips, he drew her intimately closer, harder, higher, deeper.

That was all it took.

Gripping the blankets with both hands, she cried

her release, pulling a rumbling growl from Jace's throat.

All male. All dominant, aggressive male was this husband of hers. And the thought that she could give him such pleasure, bring him to the edge of such a soul-shattering precipice stoked her urgency. Taking as much as she gave, she demanded Jace's surrender. With a final gasp, he emptied himself deep inside her.

Sated, exhausted, she stroked his back, his chest, wiping away his sweat and hers. Gazing into his eyes, bright and blue, she smiled an impish smile and tangled her legs with his.

"Hmm. Love in the afternoon. What could be any better?"

Jace settled his hand in the curve of her waist. "I can think of a couple of things."

"Like what?"

"Love in a hot, steamy morning shower. Or under a clear and cool moonlit night." He leaned forward to brush his lips over hers. "Or again. Right now."

"Liar."

He took her hand to show her he wasn't lying. "Now, are you going to let me in on this secret celebration?"

She kept her hand where it was. "What do you want for Christmas, Jace?"

"Good Lord, Eden. Christmas is eight months away." He moved against her hand and slid his hand around to cup her bottom. "I'd rather think about here and now."

"Seriously. Which would you prefer? A son or a daughter?"

His hand stopped its erotic exploration. Beneath her palm, she felt his heartbeat kick into overdrive.

"Eden," he ground out in a menacing whisper.

She ran one nail around a flat male nipple. "I was thinking another girl might be just the thing to settle Beth down. But Ben would absolutely adore a baby brother."

"Eden." This time the growl was loud. And threatening. "Tell me."

"Of course, as we both know, twins definitely aren't out of the question."

He grabbed her shoulders. "Dammit, Eden Morgan, what the hell are you trying to say?"

She caressed him with eyes suddenly misty with tears. "I'm pregnant, Jace. You're going to be a daddy."

For a long silent minute he stared unblinking into her eyes. Then he lowered his gaze to her belly and drew his hand around to cover the imagined swell.

"I'm already a daddy." His voice was gruff and low. "Beth and Ben couldn't be any more mine if I'd biologically fathered them."

Raising his gaze to hers, he added, "But seeing you grow big with our child will be a special joy."

Knowing he'd be fair, that he'd never place one child before another had never been a fear. Still, hearing him voice the words brought a sense of calm to her stomach where nerves—or perhaps out-and-out lust—fluttered incessantly.

"Then you wouldn't mind twins? Again?"

He blinked away the moisture from his eyes and ran a sexy finger in a circle over her belly. "Baby, I wouldn't mind triplets. We're sitting on acres of land. We'll just assign 'em all a little square."

His finger moved down to tangle between her thighs. "Besides, you know how I feel about pregnant women."

The grin he gave, all sexy man and naughty boy, flicked a spark onto the coals of her desire. She wiggled against him, enjoying his delight as much as his hard body. "Anyone ever tell you you're a crazy man?"

"Only you, baby. And I must be, or I would've been doing this long before now." He swooped down to kiss her long and hard, then just as suddenly jerked away.

"Oh, God. Eden. A baby," he yelled, then fell back spread-eagled on the bed. "I'm going to have a baby." He raised his chin just enough to narrow one wicked eye her way. "How do you suppose that happened?"

With a sinfully evil gleam in her eye, she straddled his reclining form. "Why don't you just let me show you?"

And she did.

Coming October 1999 From Bouquet Romances

#17 Somewhere In The Night by Marcia Evanick
__(0-8217-6373-3, $3.99) When Detective Chad Barnett finds Bridget McKenzie trembling at his door, the devastating memories of the case they worked on together five years ago come rushing back. While he can't deny the beautiful clairvoyant's plea for help, he knows he must resist the tender feelings she stirs in his heart.

#18 Unguarded Hearts by Lynda Sue Cooper
__(0-8217-6374-1, $3.99) Pro-basketball coach Mitch Halloran would have sent the gorgeous blonde bodyguard packing, but death threats were no joke—and Nina Wild didn't take "no" for an answer. But when Nina becomes the target of his stalker, he realizes she's the one woman in the world he isn't willing to lose.

#19 And Then Came You by Connie Keenan
__(0-8217-6375-X, $3.99) When attorney Cole Jaeger returns to Montana to sell the ranch he inherited from his uncle, he discovers one big problem—feisty beauty Sarah Keller, who not only lives at the ranch, but has the crazy notion that he's a rugged cowboy with a love of country life and a heart of gold.

#20 Perfect Fit by Lynda Simmons
__(0-8217-6376-8, $3.99) Wedding gown designer Rachel Banks creates dresses brides can only dream of, even if her own dreams have nothing to do with matrimony. But when blue-eyed charmer Mark Robison shows up at his sister's final fitting, sparks fly between the two.

Call toll free **1-888-345-BOOK** to order by phone or use this coupon to order by mail.

Name _____

Address _____

City _____ State _____ Zip _____

Please send me the books I have checked above.

I am enclosing	$_____
Plus postage and handling*	$_____
Sales tax (where applicable)	$_____
Total amount enclosed	$_____

*Add $2.50 for the first book and $.50 for each additional book.

Send check or Money order (no cash or CODs) to:

Kensington Publishing Corp., 850 Third Avenue, New York, NY 10022

Prices and Numbers subject to change without notice. Valid only in the U.S.

All books will be available 10/1/99. All orders subject to availability.

Check out our web site at **www.kensingtonbooks.com**